MW01611141

ROSALIND'S SEAL (SPECIAL FORCES: OPERATION ALPHA)

FINDING HOME, BOOK 7

JULIA BRIGHT

Dear Readers,

Welcome to the Special Forces: Operation Alpha Fan-Fiction world!

If you are new to this amazing world, in a nutshell the author wrote a story using one or more of my characters in it. Sometimes that character has a major role in the story, and other times they are only mentioned briefly. This is perfectly legal and allowable because they are going through Aces Press to publish the story.

This book is entirely the work of the author who wrote it. While I might have assisted with brainstorming and other ideas about which of my characters to use, I didn't have any part in the process or writing or editing the story.

I'm proud and excited that so many authors loved my characters enough that they wanted to write them into their own story. Thank you for supporting them, and me!

READ ON!
    Xoxo
    Susan Stoker

CHAPTER ONE

*D*unk slid down the rope and dropped the last foot, bending his knees to absorb the shock before he took off running to the next obstacle. The guys were at the end of the course, yelling for him to hurry as he crawled under the wicked barbed wire. He was in a race against his last time, trying to beat the course record he'd set.

No question, Dunk was in his prime. He felt like nothing could take him down. Even goofing off on the obstacle course on their last day before leave, he was setting records.

The first part of his leave was going to suck donkey balls. Distracted by thoughts of his sister's wedding, he almost fell off the balance logs. The guys whooped and laughed. He flipped them off before running the second set of hooyah logs.

Dianna, his sister, was marrying some posh dude from the UK, and they were doing a destination wedding. He'd joked about calling her Lady Di, but she'd told him not to call her that in front of her soon-to-be English relatives. According to her, they weren't the type that would take that joke well.

He wanted to see his sister, so that part wasn't bad, but the last thing he wanted to do was spend half his leave playing nice at some posh resort in the middle of the Indian Ocean. Her new in-laws were very wealthy, unlike the people he normally hung around. If it were anyone but his sister, he wouldn't have promised to be on his best behavior. For her, he would do anything.

He settled on the slide for life and started going down, accepting that he would just have to behave for the ten days they were at the resort. Then he was heading to Alaska to spend two weeks hiking and hitting on sexy women working the summer crowds.

He crossed the finish and moved to the water, taking a cup before turning and finding Vine beside him.

"Not bad." Vine patted him on the back and showed him the timer. He'd cut one second off his time.

"Next time, don't almost fall off the balance logs," Minx said.

They all laughed as they picked up their gear and headed to their space where they'd pack away everything for their nearly month away. They'd earned their time off. Two weeks ago, they'd been in Indonesia, rescuing a group of dignitaries from a terrorist who threatened to blow up some buildings. Now the terrorists were either dead or in prison and wouldn't see the outside anytime soon.

"You ready to be pampered?" Wig asked him.

Dunk rolled his eyes. "I'm going for my sister."

"Sure," Minx laughed. "You just want someone to take care of you for ten days."

Dunk had heard so many jokes about the place he was going. Not that his room would be in a bungalow on the water. His sister's fiancé was putting him up in a regular hotel room, but still, the resort was way above anything his pay grade could manage. They would be pampered with massages, foot baths, and so many other luxuries he'd never even contemplated. This wasn't a place he could bring a woman back to for a night of fun. If he needed to scratch that particular itch, he would have to rent a car to take him into town and rent a room at some cheap local motel.

Before leaving the base, they did a toast to their vacations, wishing each other good times. The guys with kids were making stops at Disney. One was headed to see the Grand Canyon, and others were headed to New York. Next year, he would get to set his vacation and do what he wanted. This year was for his sister. He was happy for her. He just had to remember she wanted different things in her life than he did.

The flight wasn't bad since Dianna's soon-to-be husband had put him in business class instead of having to schlep it in coach. A car picked him up at the airport, and the man looked insulted at Dunk's travel bag. He didn't have expensive luggage. Instead, he'd used the military-issued bag he always traveled with.

The car had a dark window dividing the back passenger area from the driver, which stayed rolled up the entire way to the hotel. He guessed the people who used this resort expected privacy.

Dianna swore up and down she loved this guy. She'd begged him not to do a background search on Lyle, her fiancé. It had gone against Dunk's nature not to investigate. The one time he'd done a basic search on the guy, he'd gotten a call from Dianna, begging him to stop looking. He hadn't wanted to, but Dunk had quit investigating. Now he was headed to a posh resort he couldn't afford and would have to play nice for almost two weeks to a guy he knew practically nothing about. He guessed that's what had him so upset. He didn't know this guy and wasn't sure he even liked him.

The driver pulled into a long, tree-lined drive. The lawns were well maintained, the bushes sculpted. The place exuded wealth.

The building was just as well maintained as the grounds, and he had to say the people working at the hotel were very nice. He took in the number of employees, the guests, how the lobby was laid out, the cameras, and the doors leading to a back-of-house area. It was painfully obvious to Dunk that he wasn't their normal client. The people who came here had millions in the bank and expected a certain level of service. He didn't mind going nice places, but he could bunk down in a motel at the side of a freeway just as easily as a nice hotel.

The woman checking him in had just handed him his room key when he heard a commotion at the far end of the lobby.

"Daniel, you made it." The shriek was way louder than anything he'd heard so far at the resort as it bounced off the walls and white tiled floor.

He turned, excitement rushing through him as he caught his sister as she jumped into his arms. It had been a while since he'd seen her. She'd moved to England four years ago, and he'd been in the Navy. The one time his ship had been in the Mediterranean, she'd been busy and couldn't come to Italy to see him. He understood she had a life, too. They kept up with calls and emails but seeing her was great.

They clung to each other for a good minute, maybe more. Daniel's emotions were high, almost bringing tears to his eyes. But he wasn't going to cry. That wasn't him. It hadn't been him for a long time.

When she pulled back, and he let her drop to the floor, her eyes narrowed as she stared at him. "Still amazes me that you're the same skinny kid I had to hide in my closet."

Their home life had sucked, but they'd survived together. "One and the same."

A group of people stepped into the lobby, and Dianna squealed. "It's Lyle. Come meet him."

Dunk pasted a pleasant smile on his face, trying to be happy for Dianna, though he knew next to nothing about this man. She'd assured him Lyle was a good man, and there was nothing to worry about, but Dunk didn't trust him.

He was being a jerk because this man was making moves on his sister, but he had asked her to marry him, so at least Dianna wasn't a sidepiece. Based on Lyle's wealth, he could provide for Dianna and any kids they had. But there was something about the guy that Dunk didn't like.

"Daniel, it's good to finally meet you face to face." Lyle opened his arms, and Dunk moved in, giving him a perfunctory hug. The man seemed small. He had some muscle tone, but it wasn't enough.

"Same, man." Dunk had to remind himself to stop judging this guy. He wasn't a SEAL, but Dianna loved him.

Dunk did notice the three bodyguards with Lyle, all packing heat. Dunk stored away the information about the men packing heat for later use. He wasn't sure what would happen, but he had an odd feeling about this trip and these people.

"We're headed to the city for the afternoon. Would you like to join us?" Lyle asked.

Dunk stepped back and shook his head. Some free time would give him an opportunity to stake out the property and get his bearings.

"No, thank you. I'm exhausted and need to get some sleep." If any SEALs heard him make that excuse, they would laugh their asses off. He could operate on no sleep, and here he was, forcing a yawn to make him appear weak.

"Next time," Dianna said as she lifted up on her toes to kiss his cheek. "Love you. We'll see you in the morning then. We're going snorkeling."

"That sounds awesome," Dunk said his goodbyes to the group and headed to his room. Dianna had texted their bungalow number to him and the entire itinerary for the trip and the wedding. They were getting married in seven days. That would give him time to get to know Lyle and hopefully drop his suspicion of the guy.

After taking a quick shower and dressing in shorts and a clean shirt, he headed out to explore the resort. About five minutes into exploring, he realized his casual shorts and shirt looked like what the employees were wearing. He blended in with everyone in the employee-only areas of the resort.

The place was nice, well run, and had cameras throughout the facility except in the private bungalow area. He guessed the wealthy demanded privacy.

Dunk had just stepped out from an employee area when he saw a woman carrying what looked to be a beach bag while pulling a small suitcase. She was tall, not too thin, just right. Her breasts were highlighted by the blue bikini top she wore peeking out from under the delicate white dress that barely reached her thighs. It wasn't really a dress, more like a robe, but not a robe. She looked good in it. That was all he could say.

Her blonde hair was pulled up in a ponytail that she'd run through the opening in her blue ball cap. Her eyes were covered with large, dark sunglasses. On her feet were blue sandals that matched her swimsuit. From head to toe, it was obvious what she wore cost a lot. It wasn't the flimsy swimsuits he saw on tourists. This woman belonged here.

"Oh, thank God," she said when she saw him. "I thought I would have to carry this stuff to my bungalow and then go back for a drink. Could you take this to number four? I'll be there in a moment."

Dunk was going to tell her to go to hell, but he wanted to investigate the bungalow area again. If he could get into one of the buildings, he would be able to look for cameras inside or just get a good idea of the layout.

The woman didn't even wait for his reply as she handed off her bags before she turned and headed back in the direction she'd come. Dunk drew in a breath and let it out just as slowly. She didn't know he wasn't an employee, and he hadn't told her he was a guest. Of course, if he revealed that he was a guest, she might tell the actual employees that she'd seen him come out from a restricted area.

Once at her bungalow, Dunk tried the door, but it didn't open. He walked around the building, thinking about hopping the fence but decided against it. The last thing he needed was to be kicked out and embarrass Dianna. She would be mortified if he got into trouble with the resort security staff. Of course, they'd allowed him to walk around in restricted areas for over an hour, so really, they were the ones at fault.

He moved to the patio where he'd dropped the bags and waited for the sexy woman to return. She had great hips and flawless skin. What he'd seen of her face was beautiful. He wondered what color her eyes were.

He didn't have to wait long, maybe five minutes, and she was there, a bottle of champagne in hand.

"There you are. Why didn't you put the bags inside?" she asked.

He moved out of the way of the door and waited for her to open it. He just wanted a glimpse was what he told himself. She didn't need to know that he thought she looked mighty fine in her bikini and coverup or that he wondered what she would look like with it off. This wasn't that type of trip. Today was a reconnaissance day, not a hit on a sexy woman day.

"If you could just leave them in the bedroom, I'd appreciate it." She flashed a smile, but it didn't make it all the way to her eyes.

He took a step closer, studying her face. That's

when her lip wobbled, and tears spilled out over her eyelids and ran down her cheeks. He couldn't stand to see her cry. He closed the distance and wrapped his arms around her, pulling her into a hug. She didn't pull away. Instead, she snuggled closer and clung to him, leaving him wanting more.

CHAPTER TWO

*R*osalind couldn't believe she was crying on this man's shoulder. He worked for the resort, and who knows what type of rumors he would start about her? But his hug felt amazing. Much better than the hugs she got from her jerk of a fiancé she'd broken up with the night before. She'd been so stupid. She should have seen it, but she'd been busy working and hadn't paid attention to Brock. She didn't think she had to. Obviously, she'd been wrong.

The stranger rubbed her back, soothing her as he spoke. "It will be okay."

The gulping breath she took sounded awful as it echoed off the tile floor. She cringed as she forced herself to calm down. She could cry later when she was alone.

"I'm sorry," she said as she stepped out of his arms. Loneliness hit like a bucket of ice poured over her head. She wanted his touch again but had no right to demand he stay with her. "You should get back to work."

His chuckle vibrated all the way from her head to her center and left her feeling like she needed to hear it again. Then he lifted his hand and clutched the back of his neck. His head tilted just a little as an "awe-shucks" smile turned up the corners of his mouth. That move weakened her knees and made her want to pull him close. He probably thought nothing of that move, but it turned her to jelly when guys did that.

He looked like he was maybe seconds from saying some hick apology, which would have sent her right over the moon. He was nothing like Brock. She bet this man knew how to do a hard day's work and wouldn't complain that he had to pick his underwear up off the floor and toss it in the basket.

"I don't actually work for the resort."

Panic raced through her. He wasn't packing a camera besides his phone, but he didn't seem to have any recording devices. She hadn't felt any wires under his shirt.

"Are you following me?"

He lifted both hands, palms facing her. "No, not at all. I was walking past, and you assumed I worked here. I wasn't going to be an ass and just leave your bags in the dirt."

Rosalind sucked in air, wondering what the hell was going on. "Wait, you don't work here?" She took in his cheap shorts and shirt, then glanced down at his worn tennis shoes. "Oh God, I'm sorry. I thought with the cheap clo—" Her face heated to a million degrees. "I'm sorry. I'm being a privileged asshole. I—"

He chuckled again, sending her libido into overdrive. Heat rushed up her chest to her face, and she needed to fan herself. God, he'd felt so good plastered up against her, his muscles flexing and bunching as he'd held her.

Once on set, she'd acted against someone with muscles like his, but the actor had been happily married, and they didn't do anything other than star in the film together.

"It's okay. I don't dress like the other guests, I guess. You're right, I shouldn't be here, but my sister is getting married this weekend."

Rosalind tried to hold the tears back but was totally unsuccessful. She didn't pretty cry either. Tears streamed with snot, and suddenly she found a box of tissue in front of her. Then the guy who she'd thought was an employee but was really a guest moved her to the couch. He sat with her, holding her hand, not once telling her to not cry.

When she finally dried her eyes, she looked up at him and almost started crying again. "I'm sorry. Please don't tell anyone I'm such a mess."

He shrugged. "Who would I tell?"

She narrowed her gaze and realized he had no clue who she was. It was refreshing in a way she hadn't expected. She didn't want to ruin it by telling him, but she needed to find out if he would betray her trust the first chance he got. He obviously wasn't rolling in money, but he was here in this resort.

"Hey," the guy said. "You don't have to be ashamed of crying. Things hit each of us differently."

"You are way too nice."

He shook his head. "Not really. I'm a jerk, like most guys."

She snorted a sharp laugh that sounded too much like a bark. A little snot leaked out of her nose, and she grabbed a tissue, mortified at how she was carrying on. "I'm so sorry. I can't keep it together."

"It's okay." His voice sounded like he meant those words. This man was too nice. He deserved someone good for him. He probably had someone. All the good ones did.

She shook her head. "My ex cheated on me for six months, maybe longer. His girlfriend is pregnant. This was supposed to be our pre-wedding trip. Stupid fucker, like I should have known. I was busy—" she didn't want to say filming, so she shrugged. "I was busy working, and I should have known something was wrong when I didn't see him for six months."

"Oh, I'm so sorry. Cheating is never okay. I mean, if I'm going to sleep with someone else, I'd tell my girl-friend and let her understand it was over, but then again, I take commitment seriously. I'd never cheat."

Her heart squeezed at the idea of him having a girlfriend. Of course, he did. This guy was hot with all capital letters. He could melt butter with a few whispered words. And she bet he knew how to use his body, too.

This was the type of man romance books and movies were written about. He could probably make her come with just a look. The idea made her squirm.

He shrugged. "Not that I've had many girlfriends. I actually haven't had a girlfriend in years. I'm usually very clear that I'm a one-night stand, and that's it."

His words perked her up. She stood, and he moved so quickly she flinched.

"Sorry, didn't mean to scare you. I just have fast reactions."

She narrowed her gaze. "What is your name?"

"Dunk." He shook his head. "That's what my friends call me. My name is Daniel. My sister is Dianna. She's the one getting married. They're in one of these fancy bungalows, and I wanted to check out the area. You know, make sure it's safe here."

Rosalind nodded, thinking this man was too good to be true. Her gaze traveled over Daniel's broad shoulders and slid down to his long legs. She imagined he could wreck her if he used his body like she believed he could.

Opportunity stared her right in the face, but she had to be careful. No one, not one single soul could find out about this. She had to play the grieving starlet to a T for the press. If anyone knew she was boffing some sexy dude in paradise, they would make up lies and say that she was the one who cheated.

Rosalind moved closer to Daniel and reached up, touching his shoulder. He stilled but seemed ready to strike. Fear slithered through her, but she wanted to get even with her stupid ex, and this guy would be the perfect rebound. He'd said he was a one-night stand type of guy. All she needed was one night. Besides, she wanted to have some fun, and Daniel looked like fun. She would spend part of this vacation eating chocolate and crying in the pool, but she also wanted the chance to ride this man.

His gaze narrowed as he watched her walk around him. Her fingers trailed down his arm, and when she stood in front of him, she placed her palm on his chest and let it slip lower until she touched the top of his shorts. Based on the intense look on his face, he understood what she wanted. Now she had to deliver the terms.

"Neither one of us sounds happy about our upcoming week. How about we do something to make it more exciting for both of us?"

Daniel swallowed, his eyes narrowing a bit. "What do you have in mind?"

"Sex. No attachments. No posting to social media, no texts to friends to tell them who you're with. No photos, no trail that ties us together."

His eyes narrowed as he studied her. After a

moment, he met her gaze again. "Are you someone famous?"

Laughter spilled out, and she moved so close she could feel his heat and smell the fresh soap on his skin. He liked being clean. That was a bonus.

"If I said yes, what would you do?"

"Nothing, probably kiss you, but I'm going to kiss you anyway. Because that's what you want this to be, right? Wild feral sex, maybe some talking, but mostly sex."

She nodded as she squeezed her legs together. The thought of this man making her come with just a look grew. He could talk to her and make her come. God, his voice was so perfect, like velvet rubbing over her nipples.

He reached up and touched her cheek. "I'm going to take this slow."

"Fast or slow, I need the distraction."

Daniel growled as he wrapped his arms around her and pulled her close. His mouth covered hers and his tongue took possession, twisting around hers like he owned her. She tried to suck in enough air through her nose but couldn't. His kiss was so powerful it really took her breath away.

His mouth released hers, and she stepped back, gasping for air. She was about to say something when he picked her up and threw her over his shoulder. She squealed as her fingers clenched his pants, trying to keep from falling. But he had her. No question, this big man could handle her and all her curves. Not that she was large, but for Hollywood, she was often referred to as a big girl. It pissed her off, but she couldn't think about that now because she wanted sex.

He dropped her gently to the mattress but didn't hesitate to yank down her bikini bottoms and plant his mouth on her pussy, licking and sucking like he understood the assignment perfectly. Without breaking contact with his mouth, he reached up and pushed her bikini top out of the way. His fingers twisted and pinched her nipples, driving her closer to orgasm.

His tongue slipped inside her pussy, and then he licked up to her clit. His tongue swirling around the sensitive nerves was more than she could take. The stimulation of his fingers playing with her breasts, his tongue raking over her pussy, his chin scruff rubbing against her thighs pushed her over the edge.

"Daniel!" her voice echoed around the room. She gasped for breath as her head spun.

A second later, maybe two, he was standing, his shirt pulled over his head. She gasped as she watched him strip. When he pulled down his shorts and underwear, her eyes shot straight to his cock.

"Oh God," escaped her lips before she glanced up and met his gaze.

"You don't have—"

She scrambled up and reached for his cock. "Don't deny me this. I want this thing wrecking me."

His lips twitched up as he opened the condom package in his hand.

"I'm on birth control," Rosalind said.

"Doesn't matter. I always wear a condom. If I don't wear one with you, I'll get sloppy. I'm not going to risk you or your safety. I'll wear a condom."

The words were so matter of fact, it was refreshing. Not one person had been this plain-spoken to her in years. She lay back, thinking he would just do what all the other men in her life had. They wanted the fantasy of her stretched out below them, like how the movies showed it. But Daniel pulled her up and turned her, sliding his cock between her legs and over her pussy. When the tip of his cock brushed over her clit, she jumped.

"Oh God, that feels good."

His chuckle brought goose bumps to her shoulders. She closed her eyes, wondering how the hell she had found this man. Her plane had only arrived a few short hours ago, and here she was naked with someone who could model for a Greek god statue, about to be fucked into the mattress.

"I'm going to slide into you. If it hurts, tell me. If you want me to stop, I'll pull out and walk away."

She nodded, wondering if this man was so considerate of all his lovers. Again, she was struck by how kind he was. She'd never experienced a man like this.

When his cock pushed against her opening, she spread her legs a little wider. He wrapped his arms around her and pulled her up as he rocked his hips. His hips were plastered against her ass, his cock filling her as he brushed a kiss over her neck.

"So beautiful," Daniel whispered against her skin.

She tried to speak, but the rocking of his hips was enough to take not only her breath but her mind, too. He drove her crazy, and she knew she would come again. It was only a matter of time.

He pulled out and changed positions just when she thought he would blow. She found herself facing him as she straddled his lap. He pumped her up and down on his cock, filling her so fully that each stroke made his cock brush against her clit.

She was going to lose it again. She cried out something unintelligible as his lips found her nipples and sucked almost half of her breast into his mouth. Then his tongue swirled around each nipple, pushing her over the edge.

"Fuck, Daniel," Rosalind cried out.

This man was more than she'd ever had, and she didn't think sex would ever be this good again. Explaining this man she wanted more would be hard. He'd made it clear this was a one, maybe two-night stand with sex being the only thing on the menu. Without a doubt, she would miss this man once he left her, and she knew he would have to be the one to go because there was no way she could walk away from him.

CHAPTER THREE

*D*unk pumped up, thinking he'd found heaven as she lowered on his lap. He didn't even know her name. That had been shortsighted. This was more than sex, and because of what he'd said and how he'd acted, she would think he only wanted sex. That was usually the case, but he wanted more from this woman.

He felt something so radically different with her. She was air, and he needed to breathe. He changed positions again, and she was under him on the bed, her blonde hair spread out on the white linen. Her half-hooded eyes watched as he rose above her, pumping into her pussy so hard each thrust made her move an inch or so up the bed.

He felt like they could solve world problems together. It was an illusion. They were just fucking, but he felt so much more.

He needed to get it together. She'd agreed to just sex. And she'd told him he couldn't talk about what they did. He needed her name, but first, he needed to lick her nipples again. He wanted her pulsing as he came.

She was close, almost at the edge again. When her fingernails raked across his back, he let go and came, shoving into her pussy so deep he could see heaven.

He didn't drop on top of her. Instead, he rolled, keeping his dick inside her as he settled on his back. She rested her head on his chest, sighing as she relaxed. His cock was getting too limp to stay inside her, but he didn't want this to end. He needed another round.

She must have felt him slipping out because she pushed up. Their gazes met, and her lips curled into a smile.

"I haven't been fucked that well ever."

Her compliment brought heat to his chest and his face. "Thank you."

She moved off him and rolled to her side. He took the opportunity to head to the bathroom and dispose of the condom. Under the vanity was a refrigerator stocked with water. He blinked, then shook his head. This place really was too luxurious.

He grabbed a bottle and cracked it open, downing a healthy amount before grabbing a bottle for her. God, he needed her name.

"Here you go," Daniel said as he stepped up next to the bed.

She rolled over, her eyebrows arched high, judging him harshly for disturbing her peace. He bet she got whatever she wanted. She seemed like the type who could command others to do her bidding, and they would gleefully fall in line. She would make a good commander. All she would have to do was flick her wrist, and everyone would follow.

"Thank you. That was thoughtful."

He uncapped the water before he handed it to her. Her eyes narrowed as she sipped, but she kept them on him while she drank. He placed his bottle on the coaster on the side table and sat next to her on the mattress. She finished her sip, and he took the bottle, placing it on the other coaster.

"You're very…nice. I don't know that many nice men."

Her voice made his nerves tingle. He wanted to hear her talk again.

He turned to look at her, thinking she looked ravishing. Her hair was a little messy now, and her lipstick had smeared, but she looked like a siren. "What do you mean?"

She shook her head. "You don't want to hear about my problems."

"Give me a try. Oh, and what is your name?"

Laughter bubbled up and spilled out like perfect champagne, all light and airy, full of hope and bright as the sun. His whole body tingled.

She moved fast, straddling his lap. The position would be perfect for sliding into her again.

"Seriously, you really don't know who I am?"

He studied her, trying to figure out who she was. He shook his head. "I mean, you're gorgeous. You have a great body. You're beautiful in a way few are. I think some of that beauty is from the inside. Like, I think you're a good person."

The laughter that came out wasn't light and airy this time. Instead, a harsh bark escaped as she stood and walked away. He followed, going out onto the back patio with her though they were both naked. He guessed it didn't matter here. They were in the privacy of her bungalow, surrounded by a tall fence and vegetation. No one would be back here other than a worker.

The private pool wasn't huge, but it was totally private, surrounded by a solid wall that would keep out even the most curious.

"When I rented this bungalow, I'd thought of the privacy because I didn't want anyone putting up drones with cameras."

The hair on the back of his neck rose. "Why would someone—"

She turned, her eyebrow cocked up on one side, her hair falling beautifully over her shoulders. He'd seen someone standing just like that with clothes on, but the face had been the same.

"Ah, you got it, didn't you?"

He didn't like this laughter that fell from her mouth. It wasn't happy and bubbly. Instead, it was flat, heavy and full of self-deprecation. He moved fast to her side, wrapping his arms around her.

"I'm thick. I don't keep up with movies or tabloids. I'm not going to sell you out. You wouldn't believe me. You have no reason to, but it's more important to keep my identity secret than yours. If we got together and my face got out into the ether, spread over gossip sites, it would ruin my career."

She leaned back and blinked up at him as she studied his face. "You don't seem real."

He shrugged. "So could you help me with your name? I really am not into TV or movies. I've caught some scenes as I walked past the guys when I've been deployed, but I really don't sit and watch with them. I couldn't tell you the last movie I watched all the way through. But I do remember the guys replaying a scene where this woman turns and stares at her co-star like you just did, and I swear to God it was you."

She licked her lips as she pulled out of his hold. "So you really have no clue who I am, and you're not just playing a game."

"No, ma'am, I'm not playing with you. I'm telling you the truth."

"So you're military. I'm guessing some sort of special forces if you're afraid of your face being plastered all over the place."

He shrugged. "Something like that."

Triumph shone on her face, making her look like an angel again. "You're a Navy SEAL."

His mouth dropped open as he stared at her in disbelief. She moved to him and lifted to her toes, her breasts brushing against his arm, making blood go south again as his cock lengthened. As she stepped back, she saw his hard dick and smiled.

"For me?" she asked as she lowered herself to her knees. Before she wrapped her lips around his cock, she looked up, flashing a lusty grin. "My name is Rosalind Steel."

Shock filled Dunk as she wrapped her lips around his dick and sucked down on him. His hand settled on the back of her head as wonder spooled through him. Rosalind Steel. Even he knew that name. Why hadn't he recognized her?

She'd been an actress for well over a decade, but she didn't look like the teenager he remembered from movies when he was younger. Instead, she looked all woman, powerful, sexy, and like a fucking wet dream. He'd jacked off to her image, like when he was fresh out of Buds, riding high on his ego. The thought of that woman in the flesh, her lips wrapped around his cock pushed him to the edge. Excitement filled him, and he almost blew when she reached up and tugged on his balls.

"Gonna come." He removed his hands from her hair, giving her the chance to pull off. She didn't. He emptied his balls into her mouth, watching as she drank him in. A small drop slid from the corner of her mouth, and he caught it before bringing his thumb to his lips, sucking away the cum.

Her eyes grew wide, and she hopped up, planting her lips on his. He held her off the ground as he pumped his tongue into her mouth, tasting both of them on her lips.

When the kiss ended, he set her on the ground and reached for her pussy. She laughed and shook her head.

"I came when you did that thing with your tongue. It was incredibly sexy."

"So you thought that was hot?"

She nodded. "I did. Would you like to get into the pool?"

He shrugged. "I could use a little cool off."

Rosalind placed her hand on his chest and looked up at him. "Thank you for being nice."

"I still want to hear what's going on and why you're so sad. I'm a good listener."

She sighed and shook her head. "I shouldn't say anything. That's how stories get out."

"I won't tell anyone. I know how to keep a secret."

Her lips thinned as she studied him. "I guess you do know how to keep secrets. I mean, that's your life, right?"

"It is. Even if you wanted to know what I did for work last week or the week before, I couldn't tell you. I just can't talk about stuff, and I don't. It's a part of me now. So if you want to talk, I won't say anything to anyone."

She blew out a breath. "First, I'm starving. How about some food? You look like you eat."

His lips ticked up in the corners. "I do."

"You eat beef?"

He nodded. "I eat everything except tofu."

"Cool." She placed a call without asking him what he wanted but ordered a steak, medium, and a burger, medium, in addition to a chicken salad with the dressing on the side. When she ended the call, she met his gaze. "It will be here in about twenty minutes."

"That's fast."

She shrugged. "I'm spoiled, and I know it. I've told people they don't have to treat me any differently than everyone else they deal with, but it doesn't work. They still treat me however they are going to treat me."

"Special treatment isn't bad," Dunk said.

"No, but sometimes I want to be treated like everyone else and not some princess. I don't deserve some of the stuff they give me."

He cupped her cheek and drew her gaze to his. "Hey, you worked your way to your position. A princess would be born into it."

He had no idea how he could talk her into making their relationship last longer than just a few fucks, but he wanted to figure it out. This woman was special, not because she was a famous movie star, but because she was the real deal.

CHAPTER FOUR

*I*nsecurities slid through Rosalind. Now that Daniel knew who she was, would he treat her differently? At one point in her life, she'd thought she could date outside the entertainment industry and had gone looking for a normal guy with a normal life, which had sucked. Her current, scratch that, ex had been an executive with an entertainment company. After he'd started dating her, he'd moved to a different company. She should have known it wouldn't work out with him when he stopped working in entertainment.

But with Daniel, she felt something special. If they'd met at any other time, she would think of ways to secure a date once she got home. But with the news of her breakup, the sharks would be looking for information on her and whoever she started dating.

A knock sounded on the door, and Daniel went to answer. He'd put his clothes on, which made him look like another employee. The man delivering the food did a double take but said nothing as he slipped outside, leaving them alone.

"That guy thinks you're an employee." She fought to hold back her laughter. "He probably thinks I seduced someone who works here. The rumors that will be spread."

Daniel frowned, and she reached out, holding onto his arm. His nostrils flared as his eyes narrowed, causing her to laugh more. His frown deepened.

She leaned in and kissed his cheek. "It's funny."

"I don't like people thinking negative things about you."

She shrugged. "It goes with the territory. People will think whatever they are going to think. I have to be above it all."

"Do you live in LA?" Daniel asked.

"I have a house in Malibu, one in London, a place in New York, and then my home in Vancouver."

"Damn, that's a lot of houses."

She nodded. "It is, but when I go to those cities, I'm home. I don't have to stay in a hotel and can relax. Someone had set up a camera at one hotel in Prague, or maybe it was Oslo. My security guard caught it almost immediately."

Daniel frowned and glanced around. "I should have looked for cameras in here."

"Oh, I had it swept. That's the first thing I do when I enter a new hotel room. That's why I was carrying my own bags. I insisted on seeing the room before I allowed my bags to be brought down. Then, when I went back for them, they were busy, and I decided to carry them on my own. Then I saw you, and you know what happened next."

His lips ticked up, and she liked how he looked when he smiled. She liked a lot about him. The comparisons to her ex were easy to point out. Unlike Brock, who'd been a sniveling pissant, this man seemed to be confident. She should have seen the signs.

Daniel frowned again. "You look angry."

"Sorry. I was just thinking about my ex."

"Tell me what happened."

She blew out a breath. "Are you sure you want to hear the sordid details?"

"What I want isn't important. You are stressed, and if you talk it through, maybe you can forgive yourself and move on instead of nursing this grudge."

She stared at him, her mouth hanging open. "You are way too nice."

Daniel chuckled as he grabbed the burger and placed it on the table in front of his chair. He moved to the refrigerator and took out a bottle of water. "Would you like some water?"

She shrugged. "I should drink water instead of wine."

"We can drink wine later. Have some water and get rehydrated."

She took the bottle and settled with her salad in

front of her. The lettuce was just right, the tomatoes juicy, and the rest of the stuff perfect, so why did she wish she had Daniel's burger?

She blew out a breath. "My ex, Brock, got a woman pregnant and has been living with her while I was shooting my next movie. Maybe it's my fault because I've been doing a lot of movies but just thought he was different, you know? He said he loved me and that he was faithful."

"How long were you with him?" Daniel asked between bites.

"A year and a half. I think he cheated before, but again I was off filming."

"Why do you think he cheated before?"

She speared a tomato and shoved it in her mouth, angry that she hadn't read the signs correctly. "I came home from shooting the movie and unpacked. When I went through my underwear drawer, there was a pair of panties I didn't remember buying. I know that's a tiny thing, but I swear they weren't mine. I wasn't going to confront him about it because I wasn't sure. He was so good after that. We got engaged a few months later."

"You didn't get married fast?"

She shook her head. "He wanted a big wedding. We were planning on getting married in Hawaii. This trip was a relaxation trip before the wedding. I'm headed to Canada and Alaska three weeks after the wedding to film a movie. I'll be gone for two months, then I'm doing three movies shot in LA on the lot. Then we had these big plans, and I'd take three years off and have a baby. God, even that is gone from my plans. I hate this."

Tears gathered in her eyes, and Daniel moved fast, pulling her onto his lap. He rocked as he held her, saying soothing words. She wiped her eyes and tried to crawl off his lap, but he held her there.

"Hey, what he did was awful. You don't have to keep anything in or be embarrassed about it. You are human and get to have human reactions, too."

The eye roll was probably too much. "Not according to the tabloids."

"Forget them when we're together. You don't have to play by their rules here." Daniel picked up her bowl and fed her a bite of salad. After she took a bite, Daniel motioned to her with her fork. "So you're traveling alone. I'm surprised you don't have anyone else with you."

The eye roll was automatic. "That's also because of Brock. He didn't like my assistant. He said the guy was too aggressive. I let him go, which was a huge mistake. I've not been able to find anyone who was decent since. I should have told Brock to go fuck himself when he wanted me to get rid of Eric, but I was stupid and allowed Brock's massive insecurities rule what I did."

Daniel fed her another bite of salad, which was good but ultimately unsatisfying. After she swallowed, she hit him with a pointed stare. "Want to know what I really want?"

Daniel moved so she could see his face. He looked so intense she wanted to capture this moment forever. If she didn't have to leave and they could live out their lives here, that would be amazing.

"What?" he whispered.

She shrugged one shoulder. "Your burger."

He set her salad bowl down and grabbed his burger plate. He held the burger while she took a tiny bite.

"No, you've got to get more in your mouth. You can open it wider. I saw you do it earlier," Daniel said.

She gasped as his reference brought heat to her face. "Oh God, you're bad."

His lips ticked up on one side. "Eat more."

"It's so many calories."

"We can go for a jog later or swim, but you need more food."

She hated gaining weight, but she wanted to eat his burger. He had steak he could eat. She grabbed the burger from him and took a huge bite. His smile made her feel better. She climbed off his lap and settled next to him, chowing down the burger and fries like a teenager.

"This is so good," she said when only a quarter of the burger was left.

"The steak is good, too. Would you like a bite?"

She eyed the steak. "It's bad enough I'm eating red meat in the burger. I shouldn't."

"It's not cakes and cookies. Just one bite."

She leaned closer to him and opened her mouth

when he lifted the fork. The steak was delicious, and she moaned her appreciation. They ate mostly in silence. Daniel finished the steak, the rest of the fries, and the salad. There wasn't anything left over.

She eyed him, taking in his muscles. "How much do you usually eat?"

Daniel laughed as he sat back and patted the six-pack she'd seen earlier. "I work out hard. I have to keep my muscles fueled. I eat probably twice as much as you, if not more."

"I just can't even comprehend eating that much."

"Well, whoever is telling you not to eat is wrong. You can't overeat and expect not to gain weight, but you're probably not getting in enough calories."

"Brock used to count my calories and tell me exactly how much each bite of food had."

"That's annoying as fuck," Daniel said.

"At first, I thought he cared. Then I realized he liked to have control. Now I think he wanted to control every aspect of my life or something like that. The guy was a jerk."

Daniel stood in front of her and leaned over, so his face was only inches from hers. "He was an idiot. You deserve better. Don't settle for someone like that again."

He didn't break eye contact, and it was a little unnerving. A shiver raced through her. His expression softened before he leaned in and brushed a gentle kiss over her lips.

"Come on, let's go for a stroll."

"Oh." She glanced around, wondering what people would think of her walking around with this guy.

"I won't do anything to make people think we're together. The resort is exclusive enough no one should be taking your photo. We'll keep to this end of the resort. Also, we'll both have sunglasses and ball caps on. I'll just look like a bodyguard."

"Are you sure you want to be seen with me?" Rosalind asked.

"Very sure."

She nodded, liking how confident she felt with Daniel. They weren't a couple, and he had secrets he needed to keep just like hers, but they were getting closer. Maybe she should be worried about how close he felt and send him away, but she didn't want him leaving. Having him near made her feel better. He was unlike any other man she'd ever dated, and she loved the differences.

CHAPTER FIVE

*D*aniel made sure all the doors and windows were locked in Rosalind's bungalow before they left the building. She told him he didn't need to lock everything, but he'd shot her a look that said he would secure the building before leaving. She raised her hands and didn't question his security measures again.

Since he now knew she was a famous actress, he felt a little more protective of her. He knew of a few SEALs and other military guys who dated famous people, and there were extra precautions they had to take. Just going out for a meal meant twice as much preparation time, and they couldn't just go to the local burger place. They had to go to places that had extra security or private lounges.

This resort was a good place for Rosalind, but there

were still people here who wouldn't respect her privacy if they figured out who she was.

"Okay, so when I first saw you, you'd just come from an employee area. Why were you really back there?"

He thought about lying, but he wanted to be open with her. "I wanted to check out the security. I don't know that I really trust the man marrying my sister, so I was in the employees' only area looking for problems."

Rosalind glanced over her shoulder at him. "You didn't do a background check?"

"I thought about it, but Dianna warned me not to. She said if Lyle found out, he would be pissed. I did minimal checking but didn't do the intense digging I wanted to. Even with the small amount of looking into him that I did, she called me and told me to stop looking."

"So you don't like what you found."

He shrugged. "I didn't find anything dirty. That should make me feel good, but it doesn't. He's filthy rich and has no skeletons in closets that I could find. I just don't trust him."

"Is it because you care too much about your sister?"

Rosalind could read him too easily. He shrugged and jogged ahead to the opening on the beach. He made sure the area was safe before he turned back to watch her step into the space. The sun highlighted her from behind, making her look like she was almost glowing. He wanted to pull her close and make love to her on the sand, but it would damage her career if someone caught her fucking a guy like him on a beach like this.

"What are you thinking?" Her eyes narrowed as she stared at him.

Again, he wondered if he should lie. Truth usually got him better results with women. "I was thinking about pulling your dress up and sliding into your magnificent pussy."

Her cheeks turned pink as she fanned herself. "You have a dirty mouth."

"I'd love to use it on you, find out how fast I can make you come, then stretch it out and see how long I can hold you off."

Rosalind shivered, and the pink spread from her face to her chest. He stepped closer, his mind on the thought of bending her over and entering her from behind. His cock was getting harder.

"We should step into the ocean and get cooled off," Rosalind said.

"Not here."

"It's perfect, shallow," she cocked her head to the side as she stared at him.

"It may be shallow at the shoreline, but it drops off fast. If you want to swim, we can head to the area next to your bungalow on the other side of the island where the current isn't so harsh."

Rosalind nodded and turned before spinning back

to him and moving close, planting a kiss on his lips. His hands were on her ass, and that was a dangerous position to be in. She fit against him perfectly and felt right in his arms. But anyone could be out on the water watching them. He didn't trust other people, and with this woman trusting him, he had to watch for more than just the usual threats.

They headed back to the bungalow Rosalind was staying at and walked out to the beach. She pulled off her coverup, and his heart sped up. He couldn't take his eyes off her. She was beautiful in a way few were. He knew she wasn't his, but for this moment, she was allowing him to stick around.

The water was perfect, the company even better. Daniel didn't show off. Instead, he watched Rosalind, making sure she never was in any danger.

After a while, she got out of the water, drying off with one of the resort's fluffy towels. He dried as an afterthought, glad the ocean water had cooled his body so he didn't immediately pop wood. He wanted her to believe he could be more than just sex. But who was he kidding? That's why they were together. A woman like her would never want a guy like him. Beyond how beautiful she was, the logistics didn't work. He was tied to his post in Hawaii, and she was a free spirit, moving from one house to another.

"What are you doing this evening?" Rosalind asked.

"My sister has dinner plans for me. Part of his family is here, and I'm meeting them tonight."

She nodded. "I planned to watch old movies and relax."

He ran the towel over his chest as he watched her. Every once in a while, he caught the sadness in her eyes, but it wasn't there all the time. She had just broken up with her ex, so it wasn't like he had a real shot anyway, but he was damn glad she was letting him into her sphere.

"Mind if I stop by after dinner?" He prayed she didn't shoot him down immediately.

Her lips spread into a wide smile as her gaze rose, but her head stayed down, giving her a sexy, almost conspiratorial look. "I'd be disappointed if you didn't." She swiped more water from her hair. "I'll give you my number."

Excitement sizzled. He had Rosalind Steel's number, or he would. God, he was such a dork. He moved to the lounge where he'd set his clothes and handed her his phone, which was open to his contacts. She entered Beach Girl as her name and then her number before she texted herself from his phone.

"Beach Girl?"

She shrugged. "Better than Beach Fuck as my name."

He caught her as she moved past him. "You're more than just a fuck."

She turned her head and met his gaze but said nothing. The sadness he saw in her eyes made his stomach clench. He turned her and pulled her into a hug as he wrapped his arms around her, kissing the side of her head.

What words could he say to heal her broken heart? He guessed there wasn't much he could say or do. She'd lived a full life before him and would return to her life after. He was just a blip, but he would be a good blip, giving her more than he took.

"When I finish with my sister's thing, I'll text and make sure you're still awake. I know this is just a fling for you, but I want to make sure you have the best fling in the history of flings."

Her shoulders rose as a heavy sigh escaped her lips. "Why are you being so nice?" Her voice was reedy thin, full of the pain of unfulfilled dreams.

He tilted her chin so they were looking at each other. "Because you have value, and I want to help you see it."

Tears trailed down her cheeks. She moved to wipe them away, but he stopped her. Her eyebrows knit tight.

"You deserve to feel emotions, even the difficult ones. Cry if you need but know I'm here for you. I'll be your sex doll and show you a good time, but I'm also human and will hold you through the worst of it, allowing you to grieve what you lost."

More tears poured from her eyes. Daniel pulled her close and held her for a moment before he led her to the place she was staying. She entered the code for the gate that led to the pool area and an outdoor shower.

He helped her strip off her swimsuit and get the sand off her body before turning her around. He slid his fingers over her pussy, giving her a great orgasm before he took off to his room.

His sister had texted once, and she was demanding his presence in fifteen minutes. He had just enough time to take a quick shower and dress in slacks. His clothes weren't designer, and he could tell the difference between what he wore and what Lyle's family had on, but he didn't care. He knew his value, even if they didn't. He also easily saw Rosalind's value. She was a once in a lifetime type of woman. Anyone who had her close and let her get away was a fool.

CHAPTER SIX

*T*he movie ended, and Rosalind wondered what Daniel was doing. She checked her phone again and decided she was pathetic. She'd blocked Brock's phone number and blocked him on all her social media so she couldn't see what he was posting, but she wanted to unblock him and spy. She shouldn't, but that didn't mean she wasn't curious.

Her stomach clenched as a wave of worry hit. How could she go from thinking she was engaged to spreading her legs for Daniel? It had seemed like the most natural thing to do. Daniel was super sexy, smart, good-looking, kind, compassionate, and a damn good fuck. She wondered why he wasn't already taken. Then again, people would wonder the same thing about her. Once the news of her breakup hit the airwaves, people would crucify her. No matter how advanced they were, people would blame her for the breakup.

They'd come up with some excuse why it was her fault. She had a life and a job and wasn't going to give it up for anyone. And why did the woman have to give up her job? She made so much more money than Brock would have ever made, but people valued what men did and devalued women's achievements. She wondered what people would think of her dating someone like Daniel.

Would she give up her life to be with him? The guy wasn't like anyone she'd ever dated before, and maybe that's why she'd always put her career first. The men she dated lacked inspiration. They were like husks, nothing of substance compared to Daniel.

Her phone buzzed, and she tried to not get too excited. But just thinking of Daniel made her hot. Sadly, it wasn't Daniel. Her agent wanted to make sure she was okay.

I'M GOOD. I'm at the resort, lying on the couch, watching old movies that make me cry.

HE DIDN'T DESERVE YOU.

MAYBE I DON'T DESERVE to be happy. Being a tortured artist has a bit of a ring to it.

. . .

GET SOME SLEEP. *SM is still positive for you. The AH hasn't said anything negative...yet.*

ROSALIND READ over the text again. She knew SM meant social media, but it took her a moment to realize AH meant asshole. That made her laugh until she cried. Her phone buzzed again, and she figured it was her agent, but it was Daniel asking if he could come to her place. She replied yes without hesitation.

A knock sounded at her door, and she froze. Could he already be here? She hit the button to call Daniel, and he answered on the first ring.

"That's smart. Always call before answering the door."

"Jesus, that kind of scared me. You came all the way over here before you knew if I would agree to see you?"

"I had a hunch," he said as she pulled open the door.

Her stomach clenched. Good lord, she'd underestimated how good-looking he was. The man standing before her in dark slacks and a white button-down was the most delicious thing she'd ever seen. It was like he'd gone to makeup and the costume department, where they'd placed him in a shirt that looked almost painted on his body. His biceps bulged as he moved, making the material strain to hold him in. His shoulders were so freaking broad in this shirt that he looked like he could carry the weight of the world on them. His dark hair had a little curl to it, and his beard had been trimmed a little, not much. But his kind eyes were what did her in. She would gladly give him whatever he wanted if he looked at her like that too often.

"Are you going to let me in?"

She stepped back, still trying to find her voice and not say something stupid like marry me. That was the wine talking or something else. She did have a venue already rented. But no, she wouldn't do that—hop from one guy to another. They didn't know each other. But she and Brock had dated for years and she thought she knew him well. Apparently not well enough to know he would cheat. She'd been such a fool.

Thoughts of Brock brought sadness so thick tears pooled in her eyes. She shouldn't be doing this with Daniel. He didn't deserve to be her rebound guy. He was a keeper, not someone to fuck and forget.

"Hey, cupcake, don't let the sadness win. Come on, let's strip out of these clothes and forget about the past."

She stared up at him, worry filling her. "I don't want you to think I fuck around like this. I don't. I mean, I've had sex with men other than Brock, but not many."

He shut and locked the door before cupping her face, his eyes full of caring. "I don't think anything negative about you. You are allowed to have flings and be with whoever you want to be with. There is no judgment from me. I see the sadness, and I want you to know I'm here for you. If you need a shoulder to cry on, I'm here. If you want to forget the world exists, I'm your guy."

"Why are you so nice?" She hated how whiny she sounded.

He didn't answer. Instead, he pulled her close and covered her lips with his, kissing away the tears. They were naked in no time, her on her knees, him doing things to her she'd never experienced.

She wasn't sure how long they lasted or how they'd made it to the bed, but she woke with him wrapped around her, his hard cock poking her in the rear.

She tried to slip out of his hold, but he woke the moment she moved. "Sorry, I need to pee," she whispered.

He groaned and rolled away, allowing her to get up. After she peed, he was in the room with her. She glanced at him, then shrugged. Brock had refused to be in the bathroom at the same time as her, so much so that he'd begun using the bathroom down the hall.

"I need to get the locks changed at my place," Rosalind said.

Daniel finished and turned to face her. "Do you have someone who can do that?"

"Yes. I'll send a note to my assistant and have her take care of it. Everyone in my circle knows I broke it off with Brock, but I can't trust that he won't try to show off and take his bimbo to my house. Hell, he probably has already shown her my closets and shoe room."

Daniel's eyebrows shot up. "Shoe room?"

She rolled her eyes. "I get shoes to wear to events. The designers give them to me. They can't be worn by anyone else because I've scuffed up the bottom. It would be rude to throw them away, so I keep them in case I need a chartreuse pair of three-inch heels in the future or plum pumps."

Daniel rinsed his mouth and brushed his teeth before grabbing her hand and pulling her close. "The shoe thing makes sense, and yes, it would be rude to throw them away."

"I could sell them, but then people would accuse me of trying to make money, and rumors would be spread that I was broke. If I give them away, I'm seen as an out-of-touch idiot who thinks homeless people need three-inch heels. I'm stuck with them until I die, then someone can donate the collection to someplace that will toss them into a box, all while cursing me for saddling them with three thousand shoes."

"What about a charity?"

She shook her head. "They don't take shoes that have been worn."

"No, have a huge event where you sell the shoes, and all the money made goes to charity."

She stared up at him, wondering how she'd been lucky enough to run into someone so smart. "I could partner with a few other actresses. That way, not all the shoes are the same size." She tapped her chin, loving his idea. "There are some shoes I want to keep. There's this pair that feels like I'm wearing house slippers, but they are these badass red heels that are total power shoes."

His laughter filled the bathroom. "It sounds like you have a plan."

She felt better than she had in ages. Maybe some of it was not being saddled to Brock anymore, but a big part of it was this man standing next to her.

The next few days were spent making love to Daniel when he had time and reading scripts her agent sent over. She'd been tagged for a new movie that would be amazing if she got the part. She had to read for the director once she returned home, but that would be an easy part to read for.

The night before Daniel's sister's wedding, he'd shown up close to ten at night, and they'd gotten busy, but he had to leave to spend time with Lyle and his guys. They had a late night since the wedding started at six the next evening.

"I've gotten used to having you in my bed," Rosalind said.

He nuzzled her neck, licking up to her ear before tugging on the lobe. "I've gotten used to sleeping with you."

"I don't want to think about what happens when you leave." She'd kept the subject at bay so far. She didn't want him to leave. She liked him too much, but she knew he wouldn't stay. They weren't a couple. He was just some guy she'd had sex with, and that thought made her sadder than almost anything else.

"We have a few days left. Let's see what happens after I'm done with the wedding tomorrow."

She was falling for this guy and wasn't sure how she would deal with it when he left. She'd known he came from a different world and had a different life, but she'd wanted to have some fun. But the fun might just bite her in the ass.

After they dressed, him in the clothes he'd worn to dinner, her in a pair of shorts and a t-shirt, his lips brushed over hers, bringing forth so many emotions that tears filled her eyes. She didn't want to cry again, but she couldn't help it.

He was about to pull back when a knock sounded at the door. "Shit, I guess my new brother-in-law found me," Daniel said.

Rosalind chuckled. "Go. Have fun. I'll see you in a few days."

He hesitated before stepping to the door. She liked how torn he was. Maybe they could figure something out where they could be together. It would be hard, but this man was worth it.

Daniel flashed her a smile as he tugged open the door. She was looking at him and didn't see the men in black before it was too late. A buzz shot through her, and pain radiated out, forcing her to her knees. Daniel went down, too, but they had a harder time with him.

Then one of the three guys punched him, knocking him to the ground.

Panic filled Rosalind. Who were these people? Not Daniel's brother-in-law. No way would they attack like this. A needle was jabbed in her arm, and everything went dark.

CHAPTER SEVEN

*a*t first, Dunk wondered what had happened, then the image of Rosalind being taken captive filled his mind. He couldn't shake the idea something was very wrong. He closed his eyes, trying to get his brain to function correctly before he popped them open and realized they were really screwed.

His hands were bound, not by zip ties, but by cuffs. Someone had bent his arms and tied his bound wrists to his chest. His legs were bound together, and they were attached to the floor. It would take a lot to get free.

He could make out another person slumped in the corner. The dim lighting kept him from knowing who was with him. He tried to move closer to get a better look but couldn't see. He closed his eyes and counted to ten before he opened them, letting them adjust to the darkness. After a little of the fog swamping him disappeared, he could make out the delicate curve of Rosalind's cheek. Anger whipped through him. He was trapped and totally impotent. There was no way he could save her.

Time seemed to move slowly. He drifted off a couple of times before he realized they were on a boat. Who had taken them?

They'd been on the boat for a while, maybe hours when Rosalind regained consciousness. She jerked awake and tried to sit up. But she couldn't move. She was just as trapped as he was.

A cloth had been stuffed into his mouth, and something had been tied around his head, preventing him from talking. She could at least speak.

"Daniel, is that you?"

He nodded and then tried to make a noise that sounded affirmative. She peered at him, then sighed.

"We're both bound, and you can't talk, can you?"

He grunted, wishing he could tell her everything would be okay. But would it? Would anything ever be fine again? They were trapped on a boat, and he had no way of getting free.

"What happened? Never mind, you can't talk. Shit, this sucks."

He wanted to laugh at her massive understatement. This sucked big time. They would have to wait until they got to land, and hopefully, someone would make the mistake of underestimating him. He wanted to tell her to get some rest, but he couldn't speak.

Being bound and gagged was incredibly annoying. Daniel hoped they didn't have to wait long to figure out who their captor was and what they wanted. If this had anything to do with him or the military, he would never forgive himself for involving Rosalind.

The engine changed pitch, and Dunk went on high alert. Not that he could do much with the bindings trapping him in the chair.

"Do you think they are stopping?" Rosalind whispered.

He wanted to hop up and defend her, but the most he could do was toss a murderous gaze toward the men who stepped into the room. They pulled Rosalind up and led her up a set of steep stairs. Dunk was about to throw a fit when they untied his feet from the floor and stood him up.

"Move. And don't try anything funny, or she dies."

They could threaten him all they wanted to, but threatening Rosalind went too far. He wanted to rip their heads off and then beat their bodies with their heads. It was a ridiculous thing to think, but he hated that a sweet and kind woman like Rosalind was being abused by these people.

He was led into a building and down a set of stairs to a basement area. He couldn't see the whole room because stacks of chairs, a few boxes, and tables blocked the far wall, but he saw Rosalind being led into a room at the end with bars across the front. They were being jailed here.

The guys forced him into a chair and tied him to it. He was no match for them as long as they kept him tied up. Once he got loose, he would destroy them, and they knew it.

First, they punched him, hitting his ribs, head, and face. After a while, they undid the gag in his mouth, laughing when he grunted in pain. They hadn't made any demands or asked questions. They just kept punching him and then laughing when they got a reaction.

A man with a mustache and large sunglasses stepped around the corner. "Enough." The one word stopped the beatings.

Dunk longed to be free so he could kill them. He would make sure they never saw the light of day again.

The guy with the mustache moved closer and bent in front of him. "Well, well, what do we have here? You have the information we want, and you're going to give it to me."

Dunk said nothing. He had loads of information, like the fact that caramel macchiatos have vanilla syrup and not caramel syrup, but Dunk knew that wasn't the type of information this jerk wanted. He probably wanted to know military positions or what the military would do in certain situations. There wasn't any way he would ever spill those secrets.

"You aren't the talkative sort, are you?" The man with the mustache walked behind him and popped him on the ear. Pain surged, but Dunk held it together.

"You'll talk. I know you have the codes, so you might as well give them to me. Lyle may think he outsmarted us, but we have you now."

Shock blasted through Dunk. What did this have to do with his sister's fiancé, or maybe now he was her husband? He'd spent a few hours with Lyle, but he didn't know that man well enough to have learned any of his secrets.

The man was back in front of Dunk, standing with his hands behind his back. "So tell me the codes, and you can go."

"I don't know Lyle well enough to know what codes you're talking about," Dunk slurred.

The man threw back his head and laughed. "You're his head of security who was with his future wife. Of course, you know his codes."

Dunk fought to hide his reaction. Did that mean this jerk thought Rosalind was Lyle's fiancé? Or did they mean his sister? Either way, Rosalind was in more danger than he'd first thought. These jerks had no clue who Rosalind was, and he wanted to keep it that way.

He narrowed his gaze and stared at the man. How should he handle this? He was trained to never give up state secrets, but this guy didn't want state secrets. He wanted information from Lyle, and they'd snagged the wrong man and woman.

Worry for Rosalind blasted through him. If he were alone, he would do things differently. He had more than just his safety to think of.

Mustache man narrowed his gaze before he pulled out his phone and hit Dunk with the flashlight. With the bright light in his eyes, he couldn't see the dude's expression, but the frustrated growl made Dunk worry.

The light was turned off, and the guy stalked away. The idiots who'd been beating on him left the area. A door closed, and then Dunk heard yelling. In any other situation, he might laugh, but Rosalind was at risk. He had to get free and save her.

The bindings were too tight. They'd done a great job securing him to this stupid chair.

What codes did this jerk want? He should have done a full background check though his sister had begged him not to. She'd threatened to cut him out of her life if he looked into Lyle. He'd done that before. Searched guys she'd been dating, only to ruin her relationships. She said she trusted this guy, that he had nothing to hide. Dunk had suspicions, but he'd respected her wishes. Shit, he should have had someone discreetly get information on Lyle. What had his sister gotten into?

CHAPTER EIGHT

Rosalind couldn't hear much, but she did hear the men beating Daniel. This wasn't a movie where the director would call cut or a stunt double would swoop in and take her place. This was real, and she had no clue how to help or escape.

The sounds of the jerks hitting Daniel stopped, and the men stalked away. Then there was yelling. As long as they were yelling at each other, Daniel wasn't being hit. She moved to the bars and tried to open the door, but it was locked. There were no windows, no fast and easy exit. Though she'd had roles that included kidnapping and escapes, none of the acting gigs taught her real skills. It had all been fake.

"Daniel, are you okay?" Silence hung in the air, and fear took over. "Daniel." She didn't shout but called out louder than the first time. She was rewarded with a grunt. At least he was still alive. The grunt wasn't proof he was okay, but he wasn't dead.

The voices grew louder, warning her they were out of the office and headed her way. Sweat dripped down her forehead and over her eyebrows. She swiped the moisture from her eyes. Her stomach pitched when she saw the men stalking toward her.

"If he doesn't talk, we'll make him," one of the guys said as he opened the door to her cell and pulled her out.

She fought his hold, struggling to get away. She didn't know where she would go. It wasn't like she could walk away and head to the refreshment tent or her trailer. Another man came over, and instead of grabbing her, he let his fist fly.

Pain exploded, taking her breath and leaving her dizzy. She gasped as shock took her air and her fight.

They shoved her into a chair and then used ropes to bind her. The lights went up, and she could see Daniel's face. Blood ran from a cut and smeared over his neck and his shirt. He lifted his head and opened the one eye that wasn't swollen shut, meeting her gaze. She gasped. He looked awful, and there was nothing she could do to help.

"We're going to play a little game," the man with a thick mustache said.

"I don't like games," Daniel slurred.

The man laughed as he moved closer to her. "If you

don't answer our questions, we'll hit her. Then if that doesn't work, we'll cut off her fingers."

Rosalind whimpered as fear filled her. She wouldn't survive. They would kill both her and Daniel.

"Listen, buddy, you can kill us both. I still don't know what you're talking about. I'm not Lyle's bodyguard or a part of his security. He's no one to me other than the jerk marrying my sister. I just met him this week, and I don't know him."

Rosalind wondered if they wanted money. She had some cash tucked away. She could give them the money, and then they would let her go. That's how it's supposed to work, right? Maybe she could convince them they didn't want whatever they were asking for. What were they asking for, anyway?

"I have money," Rosalind's voice wavered as she spoke. She hated how weak she sounded.

The man threw back his head, and laughter spilled out. Then he went very serious. The change disturbed her so much she jerked back.

The guy closed in on her and leaned over, making her angle her head so much it hurt her neck.

"Listen, sweetie, you don't have enough money. No one does. I don't need a few million. I need the codes to get me a hundred times, no, a thousand times more money."

His eyes were black as night, and a thin sheen of sweat covered his face. He looked like he was ready to lose it. This was the type of man who would destroy everything and everyone to get what he wanted.

The man jerked away from her and spun, stalking toward Daniel. She didn't want him hurting Daniel again, but there wasn't anything she could do. He wasn't asking for money. He needed codes—whatever those were. But Daniel didn't have what he wanted.

The man kicked at Daniel's feet before he turned to face her. The smile he shot her way was wicked and filled with malice. She hated this man with a passion. Why was he so mean?

"Tell me the codes now, or she loses a finger."

"I don't know the codes," Daniel answered through gritted teeth."

Rosalind's brain felt like it was on fire as she tried to devise something to save herself and Daniel. She had nothing. No one would come looking for her for at least a few days. She'd told everyone she wanted time alone, no calls, no questions. Just herself and some wine and chocolate as she recovered from the shock of finding out her fiancé had cheated.

The man stalked closer. His lips were curled up so his teeth were bared. He looked like a feral dog ready to pounce. She tried to back away, but the chair was too heavy.

Tears filled her eyes, and her throat closed as emotions whipped around her like trash in a tornado. She wouldn't escape, at least not intact.

The guy held out his hand, and someone else came

close to give him something. Rosalind tried to make out what was in his hand, but she couldn't see. Then the guy held the device up, revealing fancy gardening sheers. He was going to cut off her fingers.

"Please don't, don't," she begged. This wasn't play-acting. Fear had grown to unimaginable levels. Her stomach churned, and she would have thrown up if she had eaten anything recently.

"Stop!" Daniel bellowed.

The mustached man turned away from her. "Give me the codes!"

"I don't have any codes." Daniel's voice dripped with sorrow. He looked like he was ready to cry. There was nothing he could do. She hoped he didn't think she blamed him. There wasn't any blaming him at all. This man chose to attack, and Daniel hadn't caused it. She didn't know what hell they'd been dropped into, but this wasn't Daniel's fault.

Rosalind wanted to pull him close and tell him how she felt, but they were trapped by these jerks. "It's okay," she said in her very shaky voice.

Daniel's lips thinned at her words. The jerk in charge let a bark of a laugh escape before he moved to her and grabbed her hand.

"Stop!" Daniel yelled. "If you—"

The jerk didn't stop. The pain shocked Rosalind so hard she screamed as blood pumped out from where her pinky finger on her right hand used to be. She screamed again as Daniel roared.

The pain was too much. Her head buzzed, and she couldn't catch her breath. Then everything went dark.

When she came to, the men were carrying her back into the cell they'd put her in earlier, but this time they were dragging Daniel along behind her. She tried to follow him with her gaze, but they moved so she couldn't see. Then they dropped her to the floor, sending a wave of pain and nausea through her. Her ears buzzed, blocking out all sound. The next thing she heard was the door to the cell clanking closed.

Before the lights went out, she saw Daniel lying on the ground on the other side of the cell. His arms and legs were still bound. She had to set him free. That was the only way they might survive.

The jerks had wrapped something around her hand, but it still hurt like a motherfucker. The lights went out before she made it to Daniel's side, but she kept going. She inched closer, sticking out her good hand to feel for him. After a moment, she was close enough to touch his leg. She tried working the knot near his feet loose with her one hand. It didn't budge much.

It was more important to get his hands free, anyway, so she moved again. Doing this one-handed sucked, but if she moved her other hand, it felt like fire licked along her arm and spread through her body.

She began the slow process of pulling the knot with one hand, trying to get Daniel loose. She'd been working for about thirty minutes when he shifted and moaned.

"It's me, Rosalind," she said so he wouldn't be surprised by her touch.

Daniel moaned again as she kept working on the knot. He wasn't fully alert, but he was making noise. She almost had the knot free when Daniel jerked. She jumped, and the first knot pulled free. Now she just had to get the rest of the bindings off his arms and wrists. They'd removed the cuffs holding him at some point, maybe while she'd been out. Why had Daniel been out? Had they beaten him again?

"Sorry," Daniel mumbled.

"No, it's good. I think I've got your arms free, or the knot is loose now. Let me..." She worked on another knot, loosening the ropes more. Daniel grunted when she brushed against his ribs. "Sorry."

Daniel groaned and pulled his hands free before he sat up. "I'm fine. Fuck, are you okay?"

Tears filled her eyes, and she swiped them away. "I'm okay. We have to get out of here."

Daniel closed his eyes, and his body swayed. She stuck out her good hand, steadying him. He finally opened his eyes and held her gaze. It wasn't totally dark in this horrible place, but little light spilled in, making it hard to see his face. Mainly, she saw the light reflecting off the whites of his eyes.

"How long was I out?" Daniel asked as he wiped his face with the back of his hand. He cringed as his hand probed at the side of his head.

"Not long." She wanted to see more of him, figure out what they'd done to him.

Daniel reached for her, touching her leg first. "Are you still in pain?"

A wave of nausea hit as the pain ramped up. "I'm trying not to think about it."

"Good. This is going to suck until we can get out of here. Is your hand still bleeding?"

His concern made her heart swell with something warm. He was obviously in pain, and yet he was asking about her. She drew a slow breath, trying not to focus on what had happened. "I don't think so. I'm holding my hand up and close to my body."

"Good. How about where they hit you?"

She shrugged though she knew he couldn't see her. "It's okay."

"I don't know what will happen next. We can't bank on someone coming to look for us. If I can get us out of here, I will. So follow my lead and do what I ask when I ask."

"Okay." She wanted to believe he could get them out, but he wasn't a superhero, and this wasn't a movie set. Miracles rarely happened in real life, and they would need a huge miracle to get out of here.

He ran his hand up her arm to her shoulder, then cupped her face. "Rosalind, I will do everything I can to save you."

She wanted some words of wisdom, something significant to say, but no one had written a script for her, and she had no clue how to respond. Terror washed over her in waves and mixed with the pain pulsing from her arm through the rest of her body. Nothing was working out the way she wanted. If they got out of this, she would owe Daniel her life.

CHAPTER NINE

*D*ianna checked the time on her phone as worry filled her. Daniel wouldn't be late. He knew how much this day meant to her. When she'd told him to set a reminder to meet her at four in the afternoon for pictures, he'd told her multiple times she didn't need to worry. He would not miss out on the most important day in her life. He was walking her down the aisle and was pumped about it.

She checked the time again and then met the photographer's gaze. "Sorry. Could you do the men in the bachelor party first?"

The woman smiled and nodded. "I'm sure he'll be here soon. I'll do his photos in a bit. Don't worry, it will all be okay."

Dianna nodded though she didn't feel it would be okay. She thought something was terribly wrong. Matty, her bridesmaid, stepped into the room.

"How is it going?"

Dianna shook her head. "My brother. I don't know where he is. Could you go ask the guys when they saw him last?"

Matty came close and gave her a hug. "Sure, hon. Everything will be fine."

She nodded but didn't say anything. Everyone trying to be nice. Something was terribly wrong. Daniel wouldn't flake on her like this. Since joining the Navy, her brother always did what he said he would do. He hadn't flaked on her once. He wouldn't travel halfway around the world just to blow off her big day. Something bad had happened. She called the hotel's front desk and asked them to check his room.

After Matty left, Dianna pulled out her phone, wondering if now was the time to call the friend Daniel had given her the number for. She'd been told not to call unless it was an emergency. This constituted an emergency, right? Daniel had only been missing for thirty minutes, but he'd never been late for anything before. And this was a huge day. He was giving her away. He wouldn't miss it.

Her phone rang, and happiness filled her, but it was only the hotel, telling her Daniel's room was empty. Where was her brother? Then Matty came in, her eyebrows pinched tight.

"They said he left close to ten. Said that he was excited for today."

"Shit." Dianna pulled up the contact listed as Only

for Emergencies. This constituted an emergency. She tapped the call icon on the screen and waited. Two rings in, and the guy answered, his voice scratchy like he'd just woken up.

"Mustang here."

She froze, unsure what to say.

"Hello?"

Dianna made a little noise in the back of her throat and then spoke. "Sorry, I didn't mean to call so early, but this is…"

She heard cloth rustle like he was getting out of bed, then the sound of a door shutting.

"Spill it," he commanded.

"I'm Dianna. My brother is Daniel Wilson—Dunk. I think that's what you call him. He said if there was an emergency, I should call you."

The guy must have muted his phone because suddenly she heard the water running on the other end of the line. "What's the emergency."

"It's my wedding today, and Daniel is walking me down the aisle. He's like thirty—well, now almost forty-five minutes late. He's not in his room. My husband—soon-to-be husband said he left the men at ten last night."

"Give me the location where you are, your full name, your fiancé's name, your phone numbers, and your fiancé's information, too. I need everything, and I'll see what we can come up with."

"Thank you. I'm typing out a text right now."

"I'm glad you called. I'll get to the bottom of this. Don't worry."

She hung up and then sent the text, worry pelting her. She couldn't go through with this wedding if her brother wasn't here. Lyle wasn't a fan of Daniel. He wouldn't care if her brother didn't show up to walk her down the aisle. But she would care, maybe enough to call off the wedding. The idea made her nervous, and she would be lying to say a twist of happiness didn't slide through her. She was in love with Lyle. Why would she be happy about calling off the wedding?

CHAPTER TEN

*V*ine rolled over and grabbed his phone. "This better be good," he said as he moved from his bed to his bathroom.

"Hey, it's Mustang. I know you're on vacation, but I got a call from Dunk's sister. Apparently, he's missing."

"Missing?" Vine wiped a hand down his face. They were headed to California in two days for a week-long vacation at Disney. He didn't have time for someone on his team to have gone missing.

"Her wedding is in a few hours, and Dunk is supposed to give her away."

"Fuck," Vine groaned. "Jenna is going to be pissed."

"Hey, you don't have to do anything. I just wondered if you knew anything."

"No, man. I'll meet you at the base. I have one day I can give this."

"If the brass decides to send someone, it won't be your team, so you're off the hook."

Vine groaned. "Fuck. This is bad."

"Probably," Mustang said.

"Give me ten to get out the door, then I'll be there. I think it takes me about the same amount of time to get there as it takes you."

Vine hung up the phone and pulled up Dunk's contact information. Before Dunk had left for his trip, he'd shared his location. Not once since becoming a SEAL had Vine ever had to use the location finder when they were on vacation. His stomach clenched as he waited for Dunk's location to load. He checked the address where Dunk was staying and realized that his phone was at the hotel. That didn't make a lot of sense.

He showered quickly and pulled on clothes, praying Dunk was just drunk somewhere and nothing worse had happened.

"What's up?" Jenna asked as he stepped out of the bathroom.

"I just need to check on something. Nothing big."

"We're packing this afternoon," Jenna said as she rolled over.

"I know, Luv. I'll be back before you start packing."

Jenna sighed and pulled the covers over her head. He smiled as he slipped out to the kitchen, thinking he had a great life. He loved his family, and Jenna was the best.

The drive to the base didn't take long, and he was

with Mustang and his team in less than thirty minutes after Mustang called.

"He shared his location with me before his trip. And the application says he's at the hotel by the bungalows," Vine said.

"Let me see." Mustang held out his hand for Vine's phone.

"Which bungalow is that?" Aleck asked.

"Looks like number four maybe," Midas said.

"I'll call the hotel and ask them to check there." Mustang pulled out his phone and called the hotel. Since he had the line on speaker, they could all hear that the desk person said they would look.

"Oh, wait. That's Rosalind Steel's room. Hold on."

The woman stopped speaking, and Vine leaned in. Why did he know that name? He glanced up, and Midas lifted his chin.

"Movie star. That's why you know the name," Midas whispered.

"Miss Steel wasn't in her room this morning when the room steward showed up. He said it looked like she'd had a scuffle. He didn't stick around to see if she came in for breakfast.

"Could you send someone over to look now?" Mustang asked.

"It would be my pleasure."

Hold music came on and Mustang let go a stressful sigh. He hated the music most companies played for hold music. He rolled his shoulder, trying to let the stress go.

Pid was on a computer, typing away. He stopped typing and frowned.

"What is it?" Jag asked.

"This dude, the one Dunk's sister is marrying, there's something off."

"What?" Vine asked as he moved around the table. He knew Dunk had been trying to be open about Dianna's man, but it sounded like the guy wasn't good news.

"He has some holdings that the government is looking into."

"Shit." Vine wiped his hand over his face after looking at the first screen of information Pid had pulled up.

"He's doing something illegal," Pid said.

"It looks like he's possibly laundering money," Midas added.

"Shit, the guy is dirty." Worry for Dunk spread. Their buddy was on vacation, not on a mission, yet he was in danger. This wasn't how their vacations were supposed to go. Dunk should have been having fun, getting a little drunk, and possibly sleeping with a bridesmaid.

"Excuse me, sir," a woman said over the phone.

"Yes, I'm here," Mustang said.

"Miss Steel didn't touch her breakfast. It seems like she hasn't been in her room for a while."

Vine met Mustang's gaze. They needed to take this

information to someone higher in the ranks. Having a SEAL team member abducted while on vacation wasn't good.

"Thank you," Mustang said before he ended the call. "I'll take it up the ranks. Go home, have fun on your vacation, and I'll keep you informed."

Vine wanted to tell Mustang he wasn't going anywhere, but he knew the score. He was on leave and had a vacation coming up. He would be commanded to step away. It was probably for the best. Jenna would be pissed if he canceled their vacation. She'd been looking forward to it. He couldn't do anything official, but he sure as heck could call Tex and find out if there was more they needed to know about Lyle and what kind of person he was.

He punched in Tex's numbers before getting into his vehicle. Tex answered on the first ring.

"Vine."

"Tex, how are you doing?"

"Good. Cut the chit-chat."

"Dunk's sister is marrying some guy. There was an issue. Apparently, Dunk may have been abducted."

"Send me the information, and I'll look into it. Aren't you supposed to be in California in less than two days?"

"Yes, sir." He no longer asked how Tex knew his vacation plans or anything else.

"I'll get back to you on this."

"Mustang and his team are looking into where Dunk is."

"I'll get in touch with him. Have a good trip."

"Yes, sir." Vine hung up. Guilt ate at him, but he wouldn't be allowed to go, anyway. His team was on the sidelines for another few weeks. He trusted Mustang to find out what had happened.

Once home, he found Jenna in the laundry room. "I'm glad you made it back."

"Same." He wrapped his arms around her and kissed her neck. "Dunk is missing."

Jenna turned, her eyes narrowing as she stared at him. "Are you going hunting for him?"

Vine shook his head. "A part of me wants to, but Mustang and his team are on this. I know they'll be able to find him and bring him home. I trust them. I'll keep up with what's happening, but I won't abandon you or our vacation."

Jenna pulled him close and hugged him tightly. "I know you're worried. If you want—"

"No. I want to spend time with you and Lila. Mustang and his team are more than capable."

"Okay, but if—"

"No, I'm yours for the next few weeks."

Jenna nodded. "Since you're mine, help me put up the laundry. Lila is with Ms. Banks down the street."

"I'm glad Ms. Banks moved in," Vine said as he grabbed the laundry basket and carried it into their room.

"She has been helpful. If we end up moving soon, I'll be sad."

Vine nodded. "So far, we're staying here. I don't know what the next few years will bring. It is the military, and they might choose to send us somewhere else."

Jenna cupped his cheek. "It's all good. We'll figure it out as it comes. Now then, let's get everything packed so you can head back to base and talk to your people. I know you'll be worried about Dunk until you find out what happened."

He kissed her on the cheek, knowing she was right. He would be worried about Dunk. The man hadn't been on his team for long, but Vine didn't want any of his teammates to suffer. He just prayed they could figure out who had taken Dunk and where he was before something awful happened.

CHAPTER ELEVEN

*D*unk held Rosalind as she slept. He'd dozed off a few times but tried to stay alert enough that if someone came in, he would be ready. To do what, he didn't know. Dunk had no weapons, no supplies. He needed food, water, and maybe a few ibuprofens to take the edge off.

The sun had come up, and two tiny windows near the ceiling let in enough light he could see Rosalind. She had to be hurting. In all the battles he'd fought, the missions he'd gone on, he'd never lost a significant part of his body. He'd lost the skin at the tip of one finger and the nail. He'd been shot and had a small chunk of his thigh taken off, but those were minor compared to what she'd suffered.

He closed his eyes, praying Rosalind would be okay. He hoped his sister would raise a stink about him not being there. Her wedding was happening by now, or it had already happened. He had no idea how long they'd been on that boat. She would be pissed at him for not showing up. But would she be pissed enough to have someone look for him? His phone was in Rosalind's room, so a fat lot of good Vine's tracking software had done.

Rosalind moaned, and her eyelids fluttered. She was starting to wake up. Pain flitted across her features. Her hand would hurt like hell. He wished she could stay passed out for a while longer. Being unconscious would be her only solace from the pain.

Her moan sounded pathetic. His heart squeezed for her. He brushed the hair from her face, wishing he could take the pain from her. Her eyes fluttered open, and whatever feelings he'd had before exploded, shattering the perception he could stay apart from her.

"Hey," he whispered when her gaze focused on him.

She drew in a sharp breath and groaned. "Ugh. It hurts."

"I'm sorry. If I could take the pain from you, I would."

She sat up and glanced around. There wasn't much light shining in, but two small windows allowed in enough he could see a few feet ahead of them and a bit into the corner across from them.

"I need to pee," Rosalind said.

He nodded to the other corner of the room. "There's a hole in the floor over there."

Rosalind moaned as she stood. "This sucks."

He moved to the corner with her, checking out the space before he turned to face the other way as she squatted over the hole. He hated that she had to go through this, all because of his sister's fiancé. He didn't know exactly what Lyle had done, but it couldn't be good. He was kicking himself for not doing a full background check. Even if it was slightly illegal for him to use the military resources, he should have looked anyway.

Rosalind finished, and he took his turn using the hole. After he finished, he lifted his arms. A moan escaped his mouth.

"What are you doing?" Rosalind asked.

"Working out the kinks." He slowly changed positions, stretching out his shoulders. It hurt to bend too far to the left or right.

Her eyes narrowed at him. "Doesn't it hurt?"

He nodded but kept stretching. "If I have an opportunity to cause them some pain, I need to be ready."

Rosalind glanced around, her lips down in a frown. "Do you think they'll let us leave?"

She looked so hopeful he didn't want to tell her the thought was totally unrealistic. He feared the news would crush her, but he wouldn't lie. Instead of answering, he moved to her, careful not to knock into her hand.

"I have no idea what they are going to do. I think we'll have to be sharp and look for ways to get free."

Her frown was back in place. He didn't blame her. He wasn't happy with their situation either.

"I don't like this."

He nodded. "I know."

A shiver worked through her, and he pulled her closer. Her shoulders rose then fell with her sigh. She was being very brave for someone who'd lost a finger. He'd trained for stuff like this, but she hadn't.

"I know this is stressful. We need to keep calm."

Rosalind shook her head. "I've done a few action movies, and this is nothing like what I've experienced. In movies, I get to stop if I need a break. Sure, we have scenes that have to get shot, but when the action gets too stressful, the directors understand the need for breaks."

He wanted to take her mind off her pain and this suffering. She'd brought up movies, so he decided to ask. "What's your favorite movie you've ever worked on?"

He moved to where they'd been sitting before and settled with his back against the wall. He had Rosalind sit beside him but on the side away from the bars. It was little protection, but it was all he had to offer.

"I don't know. I liked working with Chris Pine. I know he's older than me, but he's really nice. He was funny and kept me distracted when the days were long. I've worked with a few younger actors who were great. Caleb McLaughlin is easy to work with. He's really nice and funny, too. I guess I like working with funny people. It makes the day go faster."

He nodded though he had no idea what her life was like. Acting was so foreign to him. "What about other actresses?"

"There are some amazing young actresses, but I really loved working with Jamie Lee Curtis. She's super. I met Betty White before she passed away."

He knew those two names. "How was that?"

"Betty was the sweetest person I've ever met, and she cursed worse than a sailor."

Dunk chuckled, then moaned.

Rosalind turned to look at him. "Are you okay?"

"Yeah, just my ribs. I'll be fine."

"What about you? What do you like about your job?" Rosalind smiled at him, and he swore she looked even prettier now than she had at the hotel. The pain made her forehead wrinkle, and she was dirty from being beaten and thrown into this hole, but she was beautiful. There was something about her, or maybe it was just him and some wistful fantasies since they were trapped in this cell, being held captive by some maniac. They needed water, and Rosalind needed medicine. If her hand wasn't treated soon, she'd get an infection.

"I enjoy successful missions. I can't give any particulars, but there are some missions we come home from, and it's good knowing that a family will have their son or daughter home again. Sometimes, the missions don't go like that, but I like when we win."

Rosalind nodded. "If you couldn't be a SEAL anymore, what would you do?"

The question hit hard. They were being held captive, their lives were in danger, and he could lose everything. Vulnerability wafted through him like never before. He was truly afraid. It had been years since he'd felt fear like this. Even when being fired upon and locked down in a bad position, it wasn't this bad.

"I'm not sure. I haven't thought too much about it because I'm years away from being too old to be on the teams."

"Do they age you out?"

He shook his head. "No, it's more an ability thing. I mean, there are some very fit forty-year-old guys, but things start to go once you get older. Things creep up on you if you stay longer than the first few years after becoming a SEAL. But there are a few guys who are older, and they have some great experience on their side. But it's a physically demanding job. The rest of the team isn't safe when the body starts to break down. They are very harsh about passing all the physical and mental requirements."

He fell silent as he thought about the question. A few guys he knew had opened security firms, but he didn't want to be security for someone else.

"I like woodwork. I don't think I'm skilled enough to make furniture, but I wouldn't mind doing something with my hands. Security work is the easy answer, but that can be boring. Have you ever had security guards looking after you?"

"A few times. It depends on what I'm doing. At large functions, I have to have security. I guess it would be boring standing around listening to me talk to friends. Big events are the only times I see some people in the business. Some of them are just like a huge party, and it doesn't really matter what the event is."

He met her gaze as worry for her filled him. "Nothing ever happens at those things, right?"

She shook her head. "One time, a guy threw a cream pie at an actor. He was taken down hard. But usually, the security guards do nothing."

"That's what you want, right?"

Rosalind shrugged, then winced. "I guess."

He hated that she was in pain. He needed to do a better job distracting her. "What about you? What if you had to give up acting?"

"I'd move into production in one way or another. I've been working with directors, trying to learn what they do. I've done some work producing films. Things like making sure we have financing."

He nodded. "That's cool."

"There's a lot that goes into making a movie. It's not all—"

A door slammed, and voices grew louder. Rosalind froze beside him, and fear washed over her face. He pushed her back, making sure she was covered by most of his bulk. If they opened fire, there wasn't anything he could do.

While Rosalind slept, he'd tried to find an escape. In addition to the lock, they'd chained the gate closed. The work on the bars was too good for him to have pushed them out of position. This wasn't the type of place he could break out of.

He would just have to wait until an opportunity presented itself. That needed to be soon because the longer these jerks held them, the more likely they would end up dead.

CHAPTER TWELVE

*R*osalind breathed a sigh after their captors dropped a bag of food and bottles of water into the cell where they were being held. She moved to open the water when Daniel placed his hand on hers, stopping her.

"What?" she snapped. She was hungry and needed water.

"Go slow. We don't know how long it will be before we get more. Take a sip, put the lid on, and let's go through the food and determine what to eat and when."

She closed her eyes and blew out a breath. "I'm sorry. I wasn't thinking. I'm so thirsty and hungry."

"I know."

Daniel opened the water for her, and she took two small sips, then Daniel took two. As he screwed the lid on the water, she tried not to obsess about wanting more.

"We have four apples, some oranges, a muffin, and some beef jerky." Daniel shook his head. "This is the oddest mixture of food I've ever seen for prisoners."

"It looks like a snack bag the resort hands out," Rosalind said.

Daniel lifted his brows. "Really?"

"Yes. I've been here before. When you go on a tour or go out into the city, the resort gives you a bag with water, fruit, beef jerky, and maybe a muffin or cookie."

"So the people who kidnapped us gave us a resort snack bag."

She nodded, and his eyebrows shot up high. She shrugged. "What are you getting at?"

"Isn't that odd? We were at the resort, and the people who abducted us have a resort snack pack for us?"

Her lips thinned as she stared at the food. "It is odd. Why would they have snacks from the resort...unless —" she gasped, and her gaze flew to Daniel. "It's someone who works for the resort."

Daniel shrugged. "Maybe not the main dude, but one of his guys works at the resort."

She blew out a breath. "At least we have food and water."

He nodded. "And the fruit has water in it, so we have extra water."

"I'm glad they gave us food, but I hate this."

He squeezed her shoulder. "I know. I hate it, too. We're both injured and need to get out of here."

Daniel peeled the orange and split it with her. Eating felt so good. The juice from the orange felt like heaven as it slid down her throat. They saved the rest of the food to eat later. She wasn't sure how long she could wait, but Daniel kept her mind occupied by talking about Navy SEAL training.

"It's hard work, but there are also some fun times. There was one day we were in the ocean, waves crashing into my back. I felt like hell. I was hungry as two bears. Then it hit me."

"What?"

Daniel chuckled. "That I'd voluntarily signed up for their torture."

His attitude was infectious, and she felt better. They'd both been through hell, and here he was trying to entertain her. This man was practically a stranger to her, but he'd done more to make her feel better than anyone she'd ever known. It was like he could see into her soul and know what she needed.

"Thank you."

"For what?" Daniel asked.

"Knowing what I need."

He put his hand on her thigh and squeezed. They were silent for a little while, then he picked up the bag of food and handed her the apple. "We'll split this. It will give us some water we need."

She took the first bite, almost moaning as the juice from the apple filled her mouth. She chewed slowly, enjoying every crunch. She ate apples, but she could take them or leave them, but this apple was amazing.

After they finished the apple, eating down to the core, they used the hole in the ground and then sat propped up against each other, talking until they dozed off. They ate another apple, finished the muffin, and drank more water throughout the day. It may have been two days, but she wasn't sure. All she knew was her hand hurt, she stank so bad she didn't think she would ever be clean, and she wanted to be free. If she got out of this, things would change. She wasn't sure what, but she would get her life together and be a better person.

CHAPTER THIRTEEN

*D*unk hated the look in Rosalind's eyes. He wanted to save her from this, but he wasn't sure he had the tools to get them out. She slept a long time, which concerned him. He prayed the infection wasn't getting too bad.

Maybe he could talk these jerks into getting her some antibiotics. It was doubtful they would give her any pain medicine. Dunk was thankful they'd left them alone for most of the day. If they did more torture before he had a chance to start healing, it would be hard on him.

He knew his team or another team would be looking for him if he'd been captured on a mission. He had no clue if anyone would miss him until he was due to check-in. Hopefully, his sister knew he wouldn't abandon her at the altar. He hadn't fought with Lyle, but he'd left the bachelor night because he didn't know any of Lyle's friends, and he'd wanted to see Rosalind, not spend the evening looking at strippers. He didn't want to know if Lyle had touched one of the women. That would have pissed him off, and he probably would have tried to kill Lyle.

Rosalind stirred and then moaned as she moved her injured arm. He helped her sit up and opened the water for her to take a sip. She drank like he wanted her to, but he could tell she wasn't doing good.

"Let's eat some of the muffin." Maybe getting some sugar into her blood would do her some good. He pulled out the muffin and unwrapped it, giving her a chunk.

She chewed and then sighed after she swallowed. "Do you think we'll get out of here?"

He shrugged. "Maybe."

Desperation crossed Rosalind's face. "I hate this."

His heart squeezed. He wanted to help her. Their situation was desperate. "I know. At least we're together."

She sighed again. "I would have finished all the water yesterday—it was yesterday, or have two days passed?"

"I'm not sure how long we've been here. One of the keys to surviving stuff like this is to not get hung up mentally."

"So that's all we have to do?" Rosalind rolled her eyes before she winked.

Dunk chuckled. "I know, right? So what made you want to go into acting?"

"That's a loaded question," Rosalind said.

"Tell me about it."

She shrugged. "We have nothing better to do. Here goes. I didn't want to act, but my mother guilted me into it. My sister wanted to act, but she had no ability. She overacted. Every call—that's where we audition."

He nodded. "I at least knew that much."

"Well, Sheena, my sister, would overact. She never got any parts except for the background roles. Anyway, I was at one of the auditions, and the guy in charge looked frustrated. My mom tried to explain how Sheena would be perfect for the part, but the dude wasn't buying it. Anyway, he waved his hand at me and said something like if you want your kid in acting, try that one."

"He just waved his hand at you, and then your mom decided to let you try out for parts."

"Oh, she was pissed at the guy and shoved me to the front of the room. I found out later the dude was the director. He made me do a cold read right then. I was annoyed, and the part was for an annoyed teen. I was so shitty and snarky reading that part, but he loved it. I got the part, and now I'm an actress."

"What did your mom and sister think?"

She shrugged. "My mom was happy because she deemed herself my agent and took half my earnings from my earlier work. In my second movie, I mentioned it to someone, and they were like, 'Oh honey, no,' and I learned I could fire my mom and hire someone who didn't take half my earnings."

"Wow. I bet that caused some strife."

"She wasn't happy, but eventually we worked some stuff out. She still mentions it from time to time."

"What, that she stole your money?"

"No, it's not fair that I don't use her as an agent. The thing is, if I'd stayed with her, I wouldn't have become the actress I am today. She was getting me smaller parts, and I was making less money. When I did the movie with Chris Pine, I made as much money as he did. My new agent got me that part. I had no clue how the business worked, and I learned on that movie set. It was enlightening, to say the least. Chris grew up with his dad acting, so he knew stuff, and he and his dad sat me down one evening and laid it all out. They helped me so much."

"Wow, who is Chris Pine's dad?"

Rosalind laughed. "I had no idea either. His dad shows up on set, and everyone over forty was all like, 'OMG, it's Robert Pine,' and everyone under thirty was at a loss. Anyway, there's this TV show called *Chips* about cops."

Dunk chuckled. "Wait, I know that show."

"So that you've watched, but you haven't watched my movies?"

"My parents used to watch *Chips* reruns. Who was his dad?"

"The sergeant."

Dunk thought about the show and remembered the guy. "Huh, that's interesting. I know who Chris Pine is, but I didn't realize they were related."

"So I credit my success to others. I would have had a shitty career if other people hadn't helped me."

"I'm glad you had someone helping you." Dunk broke off another piece of the muffin and gave it to her. "Eat up."

She chewed on the muffin for a while, then drank a little water. Their activities were limited. They could sit and sleep or sit and talk. He did some stretches and helped her walk around a little, but neither of them felt comfortable here. They both wanted to be free, but he wasn't sure they would make it out of this.

At some point in the night, their captors came back, banging around and making noise. The lights flipped on before he could see them. Something was different. Dunk braced himself, praying nothing terrible would happen.

CHAPTER FOURTEEN

*R*osalind tried to break free as two men pulled her away from Daniel, but she was no match for them. All they had to do was touch her hand, and her knees buckled. Tears streamed down her face as she begged for help.

She watched in horror as the men zapped Daniel again, this time taking him to his knees. The first time they hit him with a stun gun, he only paused. Her horror increased as the men hit and kicked Daniel. Then she couldn't see anymore because she was being dragged up the stairs.

"Stop!" she cried out, begging them to let her go. Surely there weren't people really this depraved. But she knew there were. She made movies about deranged people who did disgusting things, but those were fictional. This was real.

She would die if the pain got worse. Her nerves

sizzled with each touch. She couldn't imagine what she would go through if they did more to torture her.

More than twenty-four hours had passed since they'd been taken from the resort, but she imagined no one was looking for them. Who would know they were in trouble? Maybe Daniel's sister would worry enough about him to ask for help, but it was her wedding. What if she decided he didn't need help? What if she just got mad that he hadn't shown up for her wedding and thought, "screw him" instead of finding someone to search for them?

Before the assholes led her outside, the men placed tape over her mouth. Her head spun, and she thought she would pass out from lack of air. She would have hit the ground, except they had their arms hooked under hers, practically carrying her.

A black sedan sat in the lot. Was there anyone in there? The trunk popped open, and for a moment, she felt relief until they picked her up and shoved her into the small space. She yelled and screamed, but they slammed the lid, leaving her in the dark.

Fear built and whipped through her, sending tingles down her back and to her toes. She cried out for help but knew her screams weren't loud enough to attract attention. She was trapped and had no escape.

CHAPTER FIFTEEN

*D*unk dropped to his knees as they hit him again with another zap. He couldn't pass out or give up. Rosalind would die if they took her away from this place. He didn't know what they had planned for her, but it wouldn't be good.

One of the men kicked, hitting Dunk in the hip. It gave him an idea. He watched, waiting for the man to kick again. When the kick came, Dunk reached out and grabbed his leg, yanking hard. The man fell, dropping his gun when he hit the ground. Dunk liked knowing more about the weapons he used, but he didn't have time to check and see if the gun had been taken care of properly. He lifted the muzzle just enough to hit the guy to his left in the leg. The other man still standing was too shocked to respond, and Dunk got off another shot, hitting him somewhere in his torso. The man he'd yanked down was scrambling to stand when Dunk shot him in the back.

Dunk made his way to his feet, pushing the pain away as he ran toward the stairs. He burst out of the door as the men shut the trunk of a black sedan. Though he was probably at his worst and unprepared for battle, he lifted the gun and aimed.

The first shot hit true, dropping the guy to the pavement. The second shot missed. The guy turned and fired, but Dunk had moved, and the man missed.

Desperation filled Dunk as he fired again. He had no other weapons, no way to get Rosalind if he didn't stop this man.

The guy fired and missed again. Dunk raced forward, praying that man would be so shocked he wouldn't fire. It was stupid, and he was acting on adrenaline and a prayer. By some miracle, his stupid plan worked. Dunk was close enough to not miss and fired, hitting the guy in the chest.

Dunk raced around to the driver's side and opened the door, hitting the button to pop the lid on the trunk. Rosalind was trying to sit up by the time he stepped around to the rear of the car.

"Oh, thank God you're okay," Dunk reached for Rosalind, helping her out of the trunk.

"I thought you were dead," Rosalind reached for him. He tried not to flinch too hard when she wrapped her arms around his waist.

"We need to go. There could be more of them."

She pulled back, her eyes wide with fear. "More?"

"Come on. Let's move out. Once the immediate threat is gone, we can seek help."

Rosalind nodded and followed him away from the building and the terror they'd both been subjected to. They were both limping, but they were getting away. An hour later, worry still ate at him, forcing him to keep them moving even though he thought they were probably safe.

"How will we find help?" Rosalind whispered as they turned down another dark street.

Dunk had no clue where they were or if there were any nearby cities. They could be anywhere. There could be natural predators out there as well. He needed to get Rosalind to safety.

"We'll keep moving and find someone who will help us."

"What if no one will?"

Rosalind sounded depressed, and he needed to give her something to look forward to. They needed water, and they had to keep their energy up. The situation was terrible, maybe not the worst he'd been in, but for Rosalind, this had to be the worst thing she'd ever experienced. He should have taken their car, though that came with risks, too. What if the car had a tracking unit in it? He didn't want to be mistaken as one of the thugs, especially if they had someone after them. That group's enemies were unknown, but he bet there were people who didn't like them.

The road curved to the left. When they finally started on the curve, he could make out lights ahead. Rosalind hadn't seen the lights yet. He decided not to say anything because he didn't want her getting excited over nothing.

"Do you have a movie lined up?"

Rosalind's head jerked up, and she narrowed her eyelids before the fog cleared a little. "Oh, yes. I'm supposed to shoot two films and a miniseries at the end of the year."

"That's cool. Tell me about them." Dunk watched the horizon, happy to see the lights becoming brighter. It wasn't just one building, but multiple. They would find some form of help there.

Rosalind started describing the films, talking about how one was a period piece, which he had no clue what that meant until she said she would have to wear a corset. He must have looked at her weirdly because she laughed.

"It's based in eighteen ninety. I'll be a duchess down on her luck, and I have to find a man to marry me."

"I guess I'll need to start going to the movies."

Rosalind shook her head, then froze. He stopped and turned to face her. "Everything okay?"

She blinked and then pointed. "That's a city?"

"It is. Come on. Let's see what we can find."

They were about two blocks away from the first building when a car raced up behind them. Dunk rushed Rosalind off the road, thinking the trees would be safer than whoever was in that car.

"Shit, that was close," Rosalind said.

"They didn't see us. Come on, let's see if we can find a phone or something."

They were close to finding help. He just needed to get to a phone and call the one number he'd been forced to memorize. If he got through, they would be able to help.

Cautiously, they made their way to the first building, an abandoned store with a few neon lights plugged in and working. The second building was a restaurant that was closed. Maybe they could break in.

When they moved around the back of the restaurant, he found the door propped open. His heart sped up. If he got this wrong, Rosalind could be hurt. Maybe he should wait and find something better.

The sound of a car engine sent fear through him. Was that one of the jerks who'd held them captive?

"Come on," Dunk said as he moved to the door and stepped inside. There was a light, but he didn't see anyone inside.

"Do you think anyone is here?" Rosalind whispered.

"No clue, but this is better than chancing being found by someone who wants to recapture us."

An old black phone sat on the desk. He scanned the

room and silently moved to the phone, praying it worked. He just needed a few minutes, then someone would come to help them. They might have to hide, but they could conceal themselves for hours if they knew help was on the way.

CHAPTER SIXTEEN

*R*osalind glanced around the room. There were mops, brooms, and rags to wrap things up, and then she spied a bunch of bottled waters. She peeled her tongue off the roof of her mouth as she moved toward the shelf with the water.

Daniel grunted, and she looked back, seeing him nod his approval. She didn't know why that little nod made her feel so good. Did she really need his approval so much that she sought it out in this situation? Maybe need was the wrong word. She wanted his approval. She wanted a lot from him, and when he smiled at her, everything seemed better.

That might just be a reaction to their circumstances. Was she idolizing him because he seemed so amazing? He'd saved her, and now she thought he was a god? No, it wasn't that. She'd liked him before they'd been captured and terrorized.

This week before they'd been abducted had been perfect. Daniel was kind, sweet, but intense. The sex was amazing, and though she knew they weren't trying to create a lasting relationship, she'd fallen hard for him.

She tucked one of the bottles under her arm and carried the other bottle to Daniel. He took the bottle and cracked it open before handing it back and taking the second bottle. He was talking to the person on the other end of the line, explaining that they didn't know their position. They had no clue where they were or if they were even on the same island as their hotel.

If it had been up to her to get them out of this mess, she wouldn't even know where to start. They were filthy, smelly, and exhausted. Both of them were injured, but she found Daniel even more attractive than she had in the hotel.

"We'll stay in the area and stay safe." Daniel ended the call and took a huge swig of his water, his gaze settling on her.

"Can they help?"

Daniel nodded. He reached out and touched her shoulder. "We need to see if they have something for pain, and then we should find something to eat. No one is here right now, but they might come back. We need to be careful."

Rosalind swallowed over the worry and fear. She had to be brave for Daniel. He was dealing with pain just like she was. If he could do this, so could she.

"What do you want me to do?"

Daniel glanced over at a desk. "Look in the desk first. I'm going to head up front. If you hear anything, just duck down beside the desk. I'll find you."

She nodded, trying not to show the fear racing through her. Rosalind opened the top drawer and only found notebooks, papers, and pens. She moved one drawer down, and it was full of files. The center drawer was a mess of pens, pencils, paperclips, rubber bands, and other office junk. She did find a bottle with white pills in it, but she had no clue what they were.

She kept looking, trying to keep her ears attuned to her surroundings. She didn't want to face anyone. Emotions rose, almost overwhelming her. She'd never been pushed this hard before.

Daniel was handling this situation because he'd trained for it. She was out of her depths and out of her league. Why would she think Daniel would be attracted to her? She wasn't anything special. Tears filled her eyes, spilling over to run down her cheeks.

She heard the door to her left open, and fear shot through her. But it was Daniel, not some stranger. He moved to her, pulling her into a hug.

"I found a bottle of ibuprofen. If we find a pharmacy, I can get some antibiotics. Are you allergic to any of them?"

Rosalind sniffled. "How can you be so put together? I'm having a breakdown, and you're trying to find medicine for me."

He leaned back and met her gaze. "Draw on my strength. You don't have to do this alone. I'm here, and we have help on the way. Don't try to keep it together on your own. I'm here to help you."

"I just feel so inept."

"You're doing great. You're handling this whole thing very well."

She shook her head. "I'm a mess."

"Sweetheart, you really aren't. I've rescued many people, and I can say with certainty you are not a mess. You're better equipped than most. You've got this."

She shook her head. "How are you so calm?"

He cupped her cheeks. "This is my life. I've trained for this. I'll keep you safe, and we'll get out of here. Right now, I need you to take these two pills."

She nodded and held open her hand. He dropped two pills into her hand and then gave her the bottle of water she'd been drinking from. She swallowed the pills, then set down the water and reached for the bottle of pills she'd found.

"These were in the top drawer."

Daniel took the bottle and opened it, glancing in. "I don't know what these are. They could be anything. Best not to touch them. I got the pills I gave you from a bottle with a label on it. Only ingest things you know you can trust."

"Like the water from the water bottles?"

"Yes. And I found some snack bags of chips and other food up front. This is a restaurant, but we don't know how safe the food is. The chips are most likely safe. It may not be what you want, but it's calories."

He placed a plastic bag of food on the table. She pulled out a bag of chips and didn't recognize the brand, but that didn't matter. They both opened one bag, and she took a bite. The lime and salty flavor were almost too much, but she didn't stop eating. She needed the food.

Her stomach rumbled, and so did Daniel's. They both glanced up and chuckled. They were still laughing when someone coughed nearby. They froze. Daniel pointed at her and then held his finger to his lips, requesting she be silent. She nodded and moved to the corner, squatting to make herself small.

Daniel nodded before he made his way to the door. She couldn't see him because of the tall metal cabinet in the way, but she wouldn't move. He already had enough to worry about without her getting in harm's way.

The stress of not knowing made it hard to breathe. She closed her eyes, trying to calm herself. She knew even the best technique wouldn't do much in this situation to keep her from freaking out. She would have to overcome the urge to cry by depending on Daniel. He would save her. She just had to keep on believing in him.

CHAPTER SEVENTEEN

*D*unk stood with his back against the wall, waiting for the person to enter the restaurant. Maybe they were just passing by, but he couldn't be sure. It could also be the men looking for them. He hoped not. He should have taken their guns, but he'd been too busy trying to get Rosalind to safety.

A shoe scuffed nearby, and then the guy coughed again. The person sounded old. Dunk's body ached, and though he could probably survive a fight with most men, he would rather be able to subdue this person easily.

The water and chips had helped, but the ibuprofen hadn't kicked in. He needed a big meal, some medical care, and a couple nights' rest to be sure of himself. At least Rosalind was safe right now.

The door pushed open, and the old man stepped in.

Dunk had no reason to kill him, but he couldn't let this guy run out and tell his friends they were hiding there.

Once the man cleared the door, Dunk pushed it closed, reached out, and yanked the man back, shoving him up against the door. The old man's eyes went wide, and he started yelling in a language Dunk didn't understand.

"Hush," Dunk said harshly.

The man stopped yelling, and his lips turned down in a frown. Rosalind came out of her hiding place, and he wanted to tell her to move back, but first, he had to take care of this guy.

"Anyone else out there?"

The old man started speaking again, but Dunk couldn't understand him. He needed him to be quiet, so he placed his hand over the man's mouth and held him still.

"What are you going to do with him?" Rosalind asked.

He glanced around, unsure what he should do. "Maybe tie him to the chair to keep him quiet."

She nodded. "When will your friends get here?"

He shrugged again. "It could be a few hours. We need to keep our heads down and stay out of sight." Dunk moved the old man to the desk and pushed him into the chair. "Grab me the aprons."

Rosalind grabbed two, and he used them to tie the old man to the chair. The bindings weren't so tight that the man's circulation would be cut off, but he couldn't get free.

"We should go," Dunk said.

Rosalind grabbed a few more water bottles before snagging the bag of chips. They were out the door in minutes, headed deeper into the city. He needed to find a place they could hole up for a while until the US military could get someone in to rescue them.

He spied a large warehouse up ahead that looked abandoned. Part of the roof had rusted through, and windows were broken, but the door was open.

"That warehouse looks promising," Rosalind said.

"That's what I was thinking. We have water and food. We can last for a while in there. We'll be off the streets. That's the most important thing."

"Do you think they'll keep looking for us—the man who took us?"

"I don't know, but I'm not willing to risk it."

Cautiously, they approached the warehouse. They were running on fumes. Mistakes happened when people got tired, and they were both exhausted. Rosalind because of her injured hand, him because of the beatings he'd endured. Something felt off, and it was more than a few broken ribs.

They found a place to sit on the second floor where he wasn't far from a window where he could see the road. Rosalind handed him a water bottle, and he made sure she drank some, too. After eating two more bags of chips and crackers, he closed his eyes, intent on just taking a moment.

He jerked awake to the sound of men talking. Rosalind stiffened beside him but otherwise didn't move. The people weren't speaking English, so it wasn't the military coming to look for them. The people moved away, taking some of the fear he felt with them.

"Who do you think that was?" Rosalind asked.

"Maybe someone looking for us. The guy at the restaurant could be free now. This situation is all messed up. I'll do what I can to keep you safe."

She cupped his face and leaned in close. "Hey, you're amazing. You've kept me safe so far. I trust you."

His heart squeezed. He felt like he'd let her down so many times already. "I'm going to try to keep your trust."

She squeezed his arm and then sat back, closing her eyes. Lines spread across her forehead, and tiny wrinkles showed around her eyes. Her life was about looking a certain way. This would surely knock her back a bit.

He had no illusions that she would want him to stick around long-term, but he wished he could have some relationship with her after all this ended. He'd grown close to her, and it wasn't just the sex. He liked her, liked her spunk, and how she managed herself. He also liked her humor and listening to her talk. She was the type of woman he could see himself being involved with for a long time. First, they had to escape this hell, then he could deal with what came next.

CHAPTER EIGHTEEN

They'd finished their water bottles and had eaten all the chips, and still, no one had shown up to rescue them. Dunk was beginning to worry. They'd been in the warehouse for a full day, trying to remain as quiet as possible. He had to keep Rosalind safe, but he felt staying here was a mistake.

As the sun began to set, everything seemed off. He was watching through the window when he saw a group of birds already bedded down for the night take flight. His stomach tightened as he kept his gaze on the tree. Sure enough, someone moved in the shadows. He focused on the spot. There was just enough light for him to see they weren't wearing military-issued clothes or packs. Someone was coming for them.

He moved close to Rosalind. "We need to move," he whispered.

She pulled back and met his gaze, understanding

evident in her expression. She winced before she moved. They didn't have time for him to check on her hand, nor did he have the items necessary to clean her wound. The ibuprofen would have to be enough for now. He just hoped he wasn't asking too much of her. He would pick her up and carry her if he needed to, but he thought their going would be smoother with her walking.

Rosalind stood and only wobbled a bit. He reached out and steadied her. Their team needed to rescue them soon. He didn't think they would show up fast enough for them to escape whatever hell was focused on them now. They needed a miracle to escape this warehouse and find safety somewhere else.

He hated the odds. The stack of shit coming at them was too big for him to handle. He was injured and had no weapons.

He sure as hell hoped his sister knew what she was getting into. He doubted she did. Whoever this Lyle person was, he had enemies that weren't afraid to use violence.

Slowly they crept over to the stairs, trying not to make any noise as they moved. He was halfway down the stairs when he heard the unmistakable thowp-thowp of a helicopter. Was that their rescue?

"What is that?" Rosalind asked.

He wasn't one hundred percent sure the helicopter was here to rescue them. This was either going to be really great or terrible. He was hoping for great.

Dunk met her gaze. "It sounds like a helicopter."

"Ours or theirs?"

"I don't know yet." Dunk wished he could watch out the window, but they'd started moving away from the edge of the warehouse to the center. He needed to get Rosalind somewhere safe. If bullets started flying, they could be hit. It would suck to be hit so close to being rescued.

"Are we going out there?" Rosalind's voice shook.

"No, not yet. We have no weapons and no protection. I'm looking for a shielded place for us to hide."

"Shielded how?"

"Thick walls, something we can get low behind so bullets won't hit us. The higher we are, the closer we are to the edge of the building, the risk increases."

"Okay, so…." Rosalind trailed off as she moved behind him.

They had to go slow since the sun had set, and the only light spilling in came from the streetlamps. They'd just stepped off the last step of the stairs when the first of the gunfire started. Rosalind let out a shriek. He grabbed her shoulder and moved them behind a pile of boxes. He didn't know what was in the boxes or if they were safe, but he made her lay on the ground so she was as low as she could go.

The firefight didn't last long, and then he heard someone whistle. He knew that whistle, he had volleyed back and forth with the guy on training missions. Relief filled him.

Dunk licked his lips, glad for the water Rosalind had thought to grab and let loose a whistle. Rosalind jumped beside him, but he put a calming hand on her arm.

"They are friendlies."

"Oh, th-thank God. I-I don't think I could take more of that." Her voice shook as she spoke. This experience had been terrifying, and he'd been trained for it. He couldn't imagine how afraid she was.

"Let me help you up. The guys will help you get into the helicopter. You can trust all of them. They'll keep you safe."

A door opened as they made their way over, and a bright light shined on them before the light was lowered to illuminate their steps but not shine in their eyes.

"Dunk, glad we found you. We did find the trail of destruction you left at that other place," Aleck said.

He helped Rosalind over a pile of metal rods, happy to see Aleck and Pid standing in the doorway. They were about three feet from the guys when Aleck let out a low whistle.

"Shit," Aleck whispered.

"What?" Worry filled Dunk.

"You didn't say you were with Rosalind Steel. Miss Steel, we'll get you out of here."

Dunk could tell she was trying to smile, but the worry, the pain, and the stress of the last few days had worn on her.

"She needs medical," Dunk said.

Aleck nodded and helped her down the last few steps before turning to lead them to the helicopter that had just landed in the center of the street. Dunk had never been so happy to see this crew. They weren't his team, but they were great guys who would get him and Rosalind to safety.

The sound of the blades spinning drowned out any words the guys exchanged over their communication units. Pid helped Rosalind while the guys ensured he was on the helicopter and strapped in.

More relief poured in when they took off. Rosalind reached over and took his hand, sending hope through her touch. He met her gaze and held it as they flew over the water to a waiting ship. She'd faced so much in the last few days and held up so well. He felt real things for her, but he feared he would never see her again once she left his side. He vowed that he would never forget this amazing woman.

CHAPTER NINETEEN

*R*osalind jerked awake, her heart racing and her breath coming in gasps. The beeping noises around her filtered in, and she sighed. She wasn't being held captive any longer. She was at a hospital. She'd been flown to Australia and operated on just after landing.

Chaos reigned when the helicopter landed on the ship. They'd taken her immediately to medical. The doctor insisted she was flown to a hand specialist in Brisbane. She'd agreed and had been shipped off after being set up with an IV with antibiotics and painkillers.

Where was Daniel? She missed him. He had his own issues to care for, and she hadn't seen him before she'd taken off.

The door opened, and she blinked, trying to focus enough to concentrate. The person was dressed in scrubs, so it was either a nurse or a doctor.

JULIA BRIGHT

"Hello, Miss Steel. I'll inform the doctor you're awake."

"Th-thank you."

"I have some water for you." The woman held the cup, letting her drink a few sips. "Once the doctor gives her release, you can have some food. It won't be much, but I'm sure you're ready to eat something."

"Shower?"

The nurse shook her head. "Not today. The doctor will want you to wait before you get in the shower. And you won't be able to use your hand for a while."

She nodded, sad that she couldn't jump in the shower. Exhaustion pulled her under, and she woke when the door pushed open.

"Ah, you are awake. I'm Doctor Knight. I did the surgery on your hand. I was able to save your other fingers, but the metacarpal of your pinky finger was infected."

Rosalind sucked in air, sadness engulfing her. "Shit."

Doctor Knight smiled down at her. "If you'd been held longer, you might have lost your arm. I'm glad you were freed when you were. You can figure out how to do things with four fingers. You'll need some physical therapy, and you'll need to relearn a few activities, but you survived, and you're strong."

Her gaze drifted to the window, staring at the other buildings surrounding them. "How public is this?"

"So far, no one has made a statement. The hospital hasn't informed anyone, and neither has the Navy. We contacted your sister, and she's on her way here. We learned you'd broken up with your boyfriend recently, so I didn't call him."

Rosalind sucked in air and closed her eyes. When the doctor had mentioned her boyfriend, Rosalind had immediately thought of Daniel. That wasn't who the doctor was talking about. The last thing she wanted or needed was for Brock to find out she was in the hospital. It would be bad enough dealing with her sister. Brock would try to use this to his advantage to promote himself somehow. Hopefully, Sheena would be easy to deal with.

"Thank you."

"I'll be back to look at your hand around five or six this evening. Nurse Harris informed me you'd like to shower. I understand, but we need you to wait. Maybe tomorrow the nurses can bag your hand and allow you to get into the shower, but you won't be using both hands."

"Can I hire someone in to wash my hair?"

The doctor flashed her a smile and shook her head. "I'll have someone come to help. They have an inflatable basin. It's not perfect, but I'll make sure they have some good shampoo and conditioner."

"Thank you," Rosalind said. Washing her hair wasn't the most important thing, but she hated feeling so yucky.

"You're welcome." The doctor turned to leave but stopped and faced her again. "This floor is only open to people who have access. No one will come up here other than the nurses assigned to this floor and doctors who have patients. None of the other patients know you are here. Relax and sleep. Your body suffered multiple traumas, from insufficient food and water to the thing with your hand. Rest. Everything else will come with healing."

"Thank you."

The doctor left, and she closed her eyes, but the images playing through her mind were disturbing. She needed something to keep her mind occupied. She wanted her phone, but she doubted the doctor would allow her to have it even if she'd made it out of the hotel with the device. She certainly didn't want to post about what had happened, at least not yet. She needed her mind to be more settled, and she wasn't sure she wanted the whole story out there.

How much of the story could she tell? Daniel and his friends had saved her, but what if they wanted their existence to remain secret? The last thing she wanted to do was reveal too much and put Daniel at risk. She owed him her life, and she wouldn't do anything to put him in danger.

CHAPTER TWENTY

*D*unk wanted to see Rosalind before she left the ship, but she was gone before he'd finished being debriefed. Apparently, he'd found a group of terrorists. When Mustang's group had arrived at the compound where he and Rosalind had originally been held, the SEAL team found weapons a group like that should never have had. The Navy's anti-terrorism experts had been dispatched, and a network of terrorists previously unknown had been discovered.

Dunk called his sister and she told him that she was in Los Angeles. They hadn't talked for long, but she had canceled the wedding. He was headed there now. He still had two weeks of leave, and he wanted to spend a few days with Dianna.

When he landed in Los Angeles, his sister greeted him. After a long hug, she took off her sunglasses, revealing red eyes. He cupped her cheek, wishing he could take the pain from her.

"Let's get your stuff. I've booked you a room where I'm staying."

"You didn't have to."

"Oh yes, I did. Lyle owes me this."

They didn't speak much in the car though he wanted to know everything. What had happened on the wedding day? Was she still involved with Lyle?

She dropped the car with the valet at the front of the hotel, and they headed inside. She wasn't in a suite, which was surprising, but he guessed she was done with Lyle, and he'd been the money train.

The second the door shut, she burst into tears. He moved to her, wrapping his arms around her shoulder.

"I'm so sorry," she cried against his chest.

"Hey, it's okay. Don't worry."

She pushed back, shaking her head. "No, it's not. Lyle is a bad person. I'd thought he was good and honest. I thought I knew everything, but I didn't. He lied about so much. He swore he would always be truthful, and I thought I could believe him. I never should have believed even one word he uttered. He almost got you killed."

"Do you know what he was doing?"

She shrugged. "I really thought he was a good guy." She closed her eyes and shook her head, pain flashing across her face. "He was so angry when I said I needed to wait for you to show up for the wedding ceremony. I knew nothing at all, Daniel. You have to believe me."

He kissed the top of her head. "I believe you."

"He put money in my name. That's the only reason I'm staying at this hotel. I'm paying in cash, too. I didn't put it on a credit card. I took the money from the account and pulled it out."

Worry filled him. "He could come back for the money."

"It was in my account. I was stupid. Seriously, I didn't think anything of him giving me the money."

"You need to be careful."

"I know, but everything I have is in London. I don't think I can go back there. I had to sit with the FBI for hours when I showed up here. I thought they were going to arrest me."

He hugged her again before stepping back. "I need to freshen up."

"Sure. I'll order lunch. I'm starving. You still eat meat, right?"

He snorted out a laugh. At one point, Dianna had gone vegan, and it had been a joke between them ever since. "You bet."

Worry slid through Dunk as he stepped into the bathroom. After using the restroom, he texted Tex, telling him what Dianna had said about the money. He wanted to make sure his sister wasn't going to be targeted.

When he stepped out, she'd just hung up the phone.

She flashed him a wobbly smile. "We have food coming."

"Thank you. Now then, what are you going to do about Lyle and your stuff at his place?"

She shrugged again. "I don't know. I'm too scared to leave the USA. What if the British government decides I played a part in Lyle's schemes?"

Dunk's lips thinned. "Did you?"

Dianna gasped. "How could you ask that?"

"Simple, everyone is going to be asking that. You'll have to answer the question more times than you want."

"Shit, I know that. I just hate it. I'm stupid for believing in him."

He moved to his sister and wrapped his arms around her. "You aren't stupid. You trusted someone who proved to be a jerk."

"I should have known. I should have let you look into him."

He shrugged. "We may not have found anything."

"That's BS, and you know it. You and your people would have found everything, and you wouldn't have been abducted. And who was that woman you were with? Is she okay?"

He was surprised Dianna didn't know that Rosalind Steel had been taken with him. He wasn't sure if her publicity people had talked about it yet.

"They didn't tell you who it was?"

She shook her head. "No. I was worried about you. I feel sorry for her."

"She'll be fine, eventually." He wasn't sure about that. He needed to get in contact with her. Would the number he had for her work? And did he really have that number? His phone had been lost when they'd taken him. His only hope was her contact information had been saved to the cloud. Maybe he could find out who her agent was and call them, but that might be creepy. They'd made no promises to each other, but he wanted her to know he was thinking about her.

"I hope she's okay," Dianna said.

A knock sounded at their door, cutting off further conversation. They didn't say much while they ate. After he finished, exhaustion hit hard.

"You need sleep. Go to your room and get some rest. We can eat dinner together tonight."

Dunk nodded. "Sure. I'm glad you're okay."

"I will be. I just need some time. I also need a place to live. I'm not sure where I'm going to land. But we can talk about that later," Dianna said as she opened the door so he could leave.

"Call if you need anything," Dunk said.

"I will. Get some sleep."

He gave her a hug and then stepped back. She sighed and shook her head. "I'm just glad Dad wasn't here to see what happened. I know he would have rubbed my face in it."

Dunk nodded. Their dad would have been a dick

about it all. He would have probably forced Dianna into marrying Lyle even though the guy was a criminal. Dad wouldn't have cared as long as it didn't make him look bad.

Dunk showered and slept for a few hours. He was up and getting dressed when a knock sounded at his door. Panic washed over him. He regretted not having any weapons as he made his way to the door. He looked out the peephole and breathed a sigh of relief when he saw Dianna.

He opened the door, and she breezed in. "Here you go," she said as she handed him a bag.

"What's inside?"

"You'll have to look, you dork," Dianna said.

He rolled his eyes and pulled out a box for the latest and greatest cell phone. "You didn't have to do this."

"You need a phone, and Lyle can pay for it."

He flashed her a smile as he opened the box. "You need to be careful about how much of Lyle's money you spend. He could come back and try to take it."

"Legally, he has no right to it."

He shot Dianna a stern look. "Do you really think he's going to get caught up with what's legal and what's illegal?"

She shrugged. "I'm angry. I'm sure I'll stop soon, but he owes us all."

Dunk turned on the phone and set up his account while Dianna decided what restaurant they were going to order from, with him agreeing to one restaurant, then having her change her mind and agreeing to the next place. By the time she ordered, his phone was syncing to the cloud. He waited, not so patiently, as his contacts filled up. Finally, he had a chance to look at the contacts and saw that Beach Girl was in the list.

Before he could chicken out, he typed a few words and sent them.

IT'S DUNK. *I just wanted to make sure you were okay.*

HE HELD HIS BREATH, second-guessing his decision to send the text. She deserved privacy, not him asking questions.

Dianna was back with the food, and he set his phone aside. He was on edge, waiting for Rosalind's reply. Maybe she wouldn't want to talk to him. They'd had sex, so what? But that sex had meant something. At least it had to him.

Midway through the meal, his sister glanced up and winced. "I'm going to stay here another two days, then head to DC. I need to find out what I can do in England."

He was ready to head home to Hawaii. He loved his sister, but he wanted to be home. He still needed to heal and figured everything would be better at home. "Be careful."

"I will be. And I'll ask you to investigate the guy before I ever date again."

He chuckled as he took another bite of his burger. "I will always look into them from now on."

Dianna had been through hell, and he was glad he could help now. He couldn't protect her forever, but he sure as heck would try to help her learn how to be aware enough to protect herself. Every guy she got serious about needed to be looked into. She wanted to think people were nice, but he knew better.

They talked for a few hours, then he was yawning too much for her to ignore. She said her goodnights and shuffled off to her room. It worried him that he hadn't heard from Rosalind, but she was probably busy doing actress stuff.

The next morning Dianna insisted on buying his ticket back to Hawaii. She forced him to ride in first class, too. He had been ready to tell her no, but she'd put her foot down.

Dunk didn't argue. His sister felt bad enough about everything that had happened, and he wasn't going to make her feel bad about him being stuffed into a tiny seat when she could afford to send him first class.

He was happy to be home but worried that Rosalind still hadn't contacted him. It would be wrong to send another text. He couldn't spend his time stalking her. She had her life, and he just needed to get back to his.

There was a thin layer of dust on his furniture, so he began dusting and cleaning, going slower than normal. His body was healing, but he still had some issues with pain. He'd cracked a few ribs, had a concussion, and his kidneys were bruised, but it wasn't anything terrible. He would survive. Rosalind had lost so much, and he wouldn't blame her for not wanting the reminder of the abduction. He hoped she could move on, even if that meant he never saw her again except when he went to a movie theater.

CHAPTER TWENTY-ONE

*R*osalind needed someone to break her out. Her sister had swooped in to help and ended up forcing Rosalind into isolation. She'd gone from one prison to another. She should have known that the sweet Sheena who'd shown up at the hospital in Brisbane hadn't been for real. Sheena still held the same grudge that made her think Rosalind had stolen her chance at Hollywood. Sheena couldn't admit that she wasn't a good actress.

Somehow, Sheena had obtained drugs that kept Rosalind out of it. Rosalind realized the second day in the hotel something was very wrong. She was sleeping too much and had no access to a phone, computer, or any device for that matter. Sheena had even removed the hotel phone from her room, and if she tried to enter the other rooms of the suite, Sheena blocked her.

She'd even hired a guy to stay in the room during the day if Sheena took off.

Rosalind didn't even know what city they were in. Confusion seemed to take over any time she was close to getting her head clear.

By some miracle, maybe she was getting used to the pills, or Sheena was late in giving her the medicine that would knock her out, but Rosalind became aware enough to know not to swallow any of the medications.

"Are you ready for bed?" Sheena asked that evening.

Rosalind wanted to tell Sheena to go to hell, but she had a plan and feared what Sheena would do if this went on any longer. She could kiss her money goodbye if Sheena got hold of it.

Rosalind had tried to be nice to her sister. She loved her family as long as she kept them at arm's length. Having Sheena close was concerning for more than one reason.

Rosalind moved to the bed, pulled back the covers, and sat on the edge. Though she'd only been trapped in this hotel room for a few days, Rosalind imagined this was how Britney Spears had felt when her father trapped her. Her mind had been dulled by the drugs, and her thoughts were chaotic.

"Now, take your medicine like a good girl." Sheena held out the tablets, a wicked gleam filling her eyes.

Now Rosalind knew for sure one of these tablets was a sleeping pill. She made a show of swallowing the pills before setting the water on the table. She hopped up, noticing the shock on Sheena's face as she moved quickly to the bathroom.

"Sorry, I need to pee." She shut and locked the bathroom door, then spit the tablets into her hand. One of them was probably an antibiotic, but she couldn't risk being drugged up tonight. She tossed the pills into the toilet and then decided to use the bathroom since she'd told Sheena she had to.

Rosalind brushed her teeth again and washed her face. When she stepped back into the bedroom, she wasn't surprised to find Sheena still there. Rosalind did her best to act tired.

"You need to get some sleep. You know, give your hand time to heal."

She nodded groggily, wondering if Sheena was buying the act. She was a good actress and knew she could play almost any role, but this had higher stakes than any role she'd ever played before. "Sure. Thanks for your help."

"Anything for you. You are my favorite sister."

"I'm your only sister."

Sheena chuckled as she pulled up the covers to tuck Rosalind in. The last few nights, she'd fallen asleep fast. The drugs had helped with that. Tonight she had to pretend to be asleep but really stay awake.

Sure enough, her sister came in an hour later and checked on her. Rosalind pretended to be passed out, totally and completely unconscious. She waited another hour before she slipped from her bed and pulled on shorts and a sweatshirt. Slowly, she opened the door, glad her sister wasn't waiting for her, and there wasn't some man guarding the room.

Fear made her heart rate pick up and her hand throb as she made her way across the room. She hadn't seen a doctor since returning from Brisbane. Sheena had kept a tight rein on her and probably wouldn't allow her to see a doctor for fear Rosalind would let it slip she was being held against her will.

A shiver slid through Rosalind as she undid the safety latch and turned the bolt. The door made way too much noise for her comfort. Her knees shook as she eased open the door. When she slipped through, excitement blazed through her. She wasn't home free yet, but she had overcome the first obstacle.

The door closed loudly behind her, making her cringe. Sheena had to have heard that. Rosalind couldn't chance waiting for the elevator. She took off down the stairs, her brain spinning as dizziness almost took her to her knees more than once. She was racing to save her life. This felt just as scary as when she'd been taken with Daniel, but she didn't have him here. She missed him.

Someone opened one of the doors on a higher floor, and she feared that Sheena was chasing her. Suddenly there were no more stairs to go down, and she popped into a hall. Disoriented, Rosalind stood, staring at the open lobby, fearing she would never make it.

She started moving to the lobby. Each step felt like the distance was too broad. Then the elevator opened, and Sheena was there, a frown marring her face.

Rosalind shrieked as fear shot through her. She took two steps, and Sheena dashed from the elevator. There was no way she would make it to the lobby. Rosalind knew her sister would never allow her freedom again if she got in the elevator with her.

"Help!" Rosalind screamed. She screamed again, desperate for freedom.

Sheena had her by the arm, the one that hurt, and tugged her hard. Rosalind cried out as pain overtook her. She couldn't get back into the elevator with Sheena. She had to fight to get away.

Rosalind dropped to her knees, unwilling to move. Sheena tightened her grip on Rosalind's hand, causing more pain. She screamed again. Why hadn't anyone come to help?

She was about to give up hope when two men rounded the corner. They took in the situation as they moved closer.

Sheena began talking, claiming she was just helping her insane sister. Rosalind couldn't stand any more lies.

"Stop! I'm not crazy. You're holding me against my will. I just want to go home and call my friends."

Sheena gasped. "You could have called your friends if you'd asked. I'm just trying to be a good sister and help you."

Rosalind rolled her eyes, hating that Sheena would

turn on the waterworks and use every gas lighting technique she could come up with to fool these men.

"Cut it out," Rosalind said. "It won't work this time."

Blue lights bounced off the tile, and Rosalind turned to find the police entering the lobby. Maybe she would be free now.

Sheena must have realized it was over because she jerked away from the men and dashed to the elevator that had just opened. She was going up, which everyone knew never to go up when fleeing a scene.

Sadness invaded Rosalind, and she let go a heavy sigh. Her sister might have been trying to help, but she'd gone overboard, just like usual. Now Rosalind would have to smooth things over with her family and try to keep Sheena out of jail. If only Daniel had been here. She knew he would never have allowed Sheena to hold her like this.

CHAPTER TWENTY-TWO

*R*osalind spent the night and the next morning trying to say enough to get her sister help but not enough to get her locked up for good. Sheena had kidnapped her, but she didn't want the headache of having her family hating her.

It was bad enough some of her family had spilled secrets, putting the dirty laundry out there for everyone to see. Her family would make a huge deal out of this. She would never have any peace.

While talking to the police, she learned that her sister hadn't even flown her back to the mainland. They'd landed in Hawaii. Sheena admitted she had stopped here because she feared someone would help Rosalind if they went to Los Angeles.

After the police station, Rosalind caught a taxi, headed to an electronics store, and bought a new phone. Hers had been lost or destroyed at some point during the kidnapping.

While still at the store, she began restoring the phone. The guy working the desk was nice enough to help her get her account up and running using the store's Wi-Fi. There were loads of notifications from people she knew expressing concern for her.

She wanted to go home and sleep off the bad vibes from her sister abducting her and the exhaustion she was still fighting, but somehow she had to get home to LA.

Her heart was heavy, and she felt like she could cry for a month. Maybe she should have booked a flight home already, but she had an appointment with a hand specialist in the morning. She planned on spending the evening sleeping.

She was scrolling through her texts, deciding who she wanted to answer immediately and who she would wait on, when she saw one from a number she didn't recognize. She opened the note, a smile turning up her lips. Daniel had texted her. She checked the date and saw it was three days ago. She stepped outside and stared at the text again, wondering if it had been too long. He was probably pissed she hadn't texted.

She typed in Hey, thinking she would add more but hit send. Her phone rang almost immediately.

"Hello?" Her voice sounded shaky even to her own ears.

"Are you okay?" The concern in Daniel's voice made her want to cry.

She closed her eyes, sinking into the sound. "I miss you."

"Rosalind, what's wrong?"

Tears threatened, and the last thing she wanted to do was break down crying in the parking lot of this electronics store. No one knew who she was, at least not as far as she knew. Paparazzi could be set up a few hundred yards away with a camera pointed at her, but she couldn't see anyone watching.

"I'm going to be fine. Are you—no, that's silly. I'm sure you're busy."

"Hell no. I'm still on leave. Where are you?"

"This sounds crazy, but I'm in Hawaii."

"What?"

"My sister did something stupid, and I've been trapped at a hotel. I just found out this morning I've been in Honolulu."

"I'm stationed in Hawaii. Which island are you on?"

"I'm in Oahu. I'm not sure what island that is, but—"

"I'm close. I'm coming to get you."

"Hold on." She opened the application for a ride share and punched in her passcode, feeling lucky she remembered it. "Give me your address, and I'll be there in a bit."

"Are you sure? I can—"

"I'm sure. This will be faster. I'll grab a ride and be there in a few."

He gave her the address, and she punched in the information and ordered a ride. For the first time in days, she felt relief.

"My place isn't much," Daniel said.

"I don't care," Rosalind said.

"I'm dirt poor compared to you."

"Honestly, I need a strong shoulder, and someone I know is honest. That's more important than anything else."

"I'm here for you."

"Thank you," she said as she spied a car pulling into the lot. It was her ride. "Listen, I never talk on the phone in one of these shared ride things, so I'm hanging up now, but I'll text and tell you my progress."

"Okay, I'm looking forward to seeing you."

She ended the call and stepped over to the car. The driver narrowed his gaze and looked at his phone, then back at her.

"You're Kris?"

"That's me," Rosalind said as she gave him a little smile. He might have thought he recognized her, but she used a fake name in the application, and she wasn't wearing makeup. Her disguise wasn't foolproof, but it wasn't terrible. She'd fooled more than a few fans going sans makeup and wearing a ball cap. The disguise wouldn't fool the best of the paparazzi or her mega fans, but it was good enough for this.

She slid into the back seat and made sure her hat

was low, blocking the view of her face before she strapped in.

"I hope you've had a good day. I'll get you to your destination in about twenty minutes as long as the traffic stays clear."

"Thank you," Rosalind said before she began texting Daniel while she worked on getting new credit cards issued.

She was excited to see Daniel. Since she was in a car with a stranger, their texts were mostly about what food she wanted and whether she wanted to go to the beach.

Being a pest wasn't her style, but after being held captive first by terrorists and then by her sister, she wasn't sure what her style was. She'd had too many things go wrong, too much strife, too much violence around her, and now she was heading to the one person who had shared her position in a huge chunk of that violence.

Excitement rose as they drew closer to his place. It hadn't taken long since there'd only been one slow-down on the freeway. The driver took an exit, and she noticed the houses were small and stacked close together. They'd filmed in areas like this on various movies, but she'd never lived in a neighborhood with houses this small and close.

She thanked the driver as the car stopped for her to hop out. Rosalind made sure to give him a big tip. He might have recognized her, and she didn't want him telling stories of how she didn't tip. Before she was two steps away from the car, Daniel was there, his arms open wide.

She went to him, sinking into the comfort that was his hug. Tears came, and she clung even harder to him.

"Let's get you inside."

"Thank you," she choked out through the tears and emotions. She needed to get her life together.

"It's not much," Daniel said before he opened the door.

"Please don't. I'm happy to be with you."

"You're a good person, Rosalind."

She snorted out a laugh. "My sister doesn't think so."

"So you have to tell me what happened. It doesn't sound good."

They stepped in, and she took in the small space, thinking it fit him. There wasn't much extra, and it was well kept. Nothing looked out of place.

"This is my home," Daniel said.

She turned and met his gaze. "Thank you for letting me come here."

He gave a sharp nod, then his lips thinned, and a determined look filled his face. "What happened with your sister?"

Rosalind blew out a breath. "Can we order a pizza and get something to drink before we start talking?"

"Sure."

With the pizza ordered, they sat at his kitchen table,

sipping iced tea. Rosalind blew out a breath and shook her head. "I thought Sheena had gotten over her jealousy. The doctor in Brisbane got in touch with her, and Sheena said she would fly over and help. I didn't say anything though I had doubts that Sheena would help without expecting anything."

"I'm sorry you have to put up with her."

"Yeah. Apparently, Sheena decided she was going to take my money. But she made a huge mistake. She flew us here, afraid someone in Los Angeles would recognize me. She thought she could check me into a hotel, drain my accounts, and take off. But I lost all my credit cards, I didn't have my phone, and she didn't get one for me, and my bank doesn't operate over here."

Daniel reached out and took her good hand. "Are you okay?"

She shrugged. "I'm hungry and tired. I have a doctor's appointment tomorrow to check my hand, but otherwise, I'm fine. I'm just sad my sister did this. I would have given her money if she'd asked, but she didn't want help. She wanted to be me."

"I'm off for another few weeks, so we can take care of your errands tomorrow."

She nodded, feeling a little self-conscious. "Is there any way I could have my documents delivered here?"

He shrugged and nodded. "Sure. I mean, why not?"

"It's just my driver's license, bank card, and some other things. I just…"

Daniel's face relaxed, and the look in his eyes made her warm. "What?"

"I don't want to be alone. I mean, if it's okay with you, I'd like to spend some time, you know, just hanging out."

"Sure. I'll take you to your appointment tomorrow."

"Oh, you don't—"

"I'm taking you tomorrow. Don't second guess me. I want to spend time with you, and that means spending time with you. I want you here in my place. We'll hang out together."

She leaned in close to him and was about to kiss him when a knock sounded at the door. He gave her a quick peck before hopping up to answer the door. She was conscious that someone might recognize her so she turned so the delivery person couldn't tell who she was.

"Thanks, man," Daniel said, then shut the door.

Daniel had a pizza box in his hands when she turned back around. She sighed and got up.

"That smells delicious.

"The pizza is excellent."

"I'm sure I'll love it."

She felt comfortable with Daniel. He had this way about him that just fit her. She didn't feel pressured to always look a certain way or like he was trying to show her off like something he'd won or bought. She could get used to being with Daniel. She just had to figure out how to get her life to fit with his.

CHAPTER TWENTY-THREE

Spending time with Rosalind was like spending time with a really good friend. She was very sexy, and he would be lying to say he didn't want her, but they hadn't tried anything last night, and he didn't want to push her today.

The doctor declared her hand fine. He removed the stitches and asked if she would be in Hawaii long enough to start physical therapy.

Rosalind didn't even glance his way before she said, "I'll be here a while."

"Good. I'll get you set up with your first appointment. It will be difficult, and if you head back to California, you need to continue seeing a doctor and find a good therapist. You will have to relearn more than just how to do simple tasks. Not having the bones on the outside of your hand will affect more than you think."

She nodded. "The doctor in Brisbane said something that stuck with me."

"What was that?"

"She said the infection was on the verge of spreading, and I'm lucky I didn't lose my arm."

The doctor nodded. "You are lucky you didn't lose more. If the infection had spread, you could have lost your hand. This is manageable. It's not optimal, but it's better than the alternative."

Dunk didn't say anything, but he was thinking it. The alternative had been death. They could have both ended up dead. Their lives could have been cut short.

The doctor walked out, and Dunk moved closer to Rosalind, hugging her from the side. She glanced up at him, and their gazes connected. He felt something go straight through him, and he swore she felt it, too. Suddenly she was in his arms, her body plastered against him.

They heard the doctor coming back, and she pulled away, but not before she kissed his jaw. She made him feel so good, and he was unprepared for how intense the emotions were. Maybe they weren't meant to be together, but he had never felt this way about anyone before.

"I sent a note to your doctor in Brisbane. She'll be happy to hear of your progress. And I have arranged for you to get some physical therapy. It's going to be hard work, but after seeing a few of the movies you've been in, I know you're used to working hard. If you're still around in a month, I'd like to check out your hand and make sure everything is healing correctly."

"Sure. I'm supposed to be on set in Canada in about a month, but I'll make an appointment before I fly out."

"Good, good. I'll see you then."

Dunk felt like cold water had been poured over him. Of course, Rosalind would keep working. That's what she did. He would be pissed if she told him he had to stop working. She turned and must have seen the shock on his face because she moved in close and lifted up to brush her lips over his.

"We can talk about it this afternoon. I mean, we need to. Neither of us knows what will happen next, but I—"

The door opened, and the nurse stepped in. "I have a script for you to fill."

"Thank you," Rosalind said.

"We've set you up with your first two appointments at the physical therapist's office. The first one is in the morning. Syd at the front desk can help with your next appointment with the doctor. Have a good day."

The nurse left, and Rosalind flashed Dunk a smile. "We got off easy."

Dunk narrowed his gaze at her and frowned. "What does that mean?"

"People who know who I am react one of two ways. Either I'm no big deal to them, or I'm the only thing they've ever wanted to meet. This was easy. The next place may not be so easy."

"Well, I'm here, so they need to keep their distance from you."

Her laughter shot straight through him. "We'll discuss that later. For now, how about we get some coffee and head home?"

"Sure. There's a great place on the way."

When they got to the strip mall with the coffee place, he told Rosalind not to open her door before he came around, and she agreed. She said it hurt to use her hand, and she didn't mind waiting. He opened her door just as a group of teenage girls were headed into the coffee shop, and one of them stopped dead still. She covered her mouth as her eyes got really huge. Dunk sensed danger, but Rosalind put her hand on his arm and got his attention.

"It's okay," she said low enough only he could hear.

The girls were jumping up and down and screaming between talking ninety miles an hour. She turned back to him and flashed a huge smile. "Could you get me a vanilla iced coffee?"

Dunk narrowed his gaze and then shook his head. "Ladies, let's get Rosalind inside, then you can talk to her. I just don't have other security detail with us."

The girls sobered, and one of them spoke. "Yes, sir."

He moved them inside and ordered the coffee and a sandwich for him. Before the woman finished with the coffee, he added another sandwich. Rosalind had to be hungry. After she got a photo with the group, he heard her telling the girls that she'd been injured, and she hadn't used a pen since being injured, and she wasn't sure if she could. She was still talking when he came over.

"I know it sounds lame, but it was really bad," Rosalind said as she held up her hand. The doctor had wrapped up her hand again, telling her she could take the bandage off while she was at home, but he didn't want her accidentally banging the side and bruising the bones.

"Oh no, what happened?"

"Was it on set?" one of the girls asked.

"I heard you were in a car wreck. Is that why there was a photo of you with the police?"

Dunk hadn't seen the photo with the cops, but he didn't think now was the time to reveal what had happened.

"Ladies, I have to steal Rosalind away. She's due at another appointment soon."

"It was nice to meet you," they called out.

Dunk led her outside, and she grabbed her coffee and took a sip. "Mmm, that's good."

They were in the car and heading back to his place when he realized she hadn't said anything. He glanced over, seeing a blank look in her eyes. "Are you okay?"

She blew out a breath. "Sorry. That was just intense. I wasn't prepared to run into fans. I should be, but that was almost too much."

"Do you think they'll tell anyone?"

"Oh, it's going to be all over the internet in a few hours that I'm in Hawaii. Good thinking pointing out the security stuff. They won't think you're my boyfriend."

Dunk turned onto the street where he lived, worry clawing a hole through his stomach. "Am I?"

She waited until he pulled into the driveway. "I don't know if you want to be. My life is complex. People will hound you. I have filming in a few weeks, and I won't be here every day. I'll be talked about in magazines."

His stomach tightened. Was this her way of dumping him? He didn't want to look desperate, but he was feeling it. If she left, he would be crushed, but there was no way a woman like Rosalind would pick him for anything other than a fling. "Let's go inside, and you can eat."

Rosalind glanced at the bag Dunk held up. "You got me food?"

"Of course. I figured you were hungry."

"I want to jump over the console and kiss you until we can't breathe, but someone will get a photo."

His cock woke up at her words. He was falling for this woman. "Let's go inside first, then we can figure out what to do."

"Thank you," she said before he could get out of the car.

"Hang tight. I'll be over there in a moment."

He couldn't believe his luck. He was dating an incredibly sexy woman, and she thought her life and job would be something that discouraged him. He wanted her more than ever before. Maybe they wouldn't make it, but if she was willing, they would give this a go.

CHAPTER TWENTY-FOUR

They stepped inside, and Rosalind moved to the kitchen and set down her drink before she walked over to Daniel and flattened her palm on his chest. It felt weird having to use her left hand for everything. She wanted to heal and get better, but right now, she wished she had the use of both hands.

"Listen here, mister, I'm feeling things for you that I haven't felt before. I know I was engaged, but that was nothing compared to this. I don't even know why I've dated other men before you. You've changed everything. You're all I can think about. I make more money than you do. That's just facts. Sure, my agent gets some, and I usually have assistants, but I'm between them because of Brock. But I'll always have people who work for me. It's just how it is. I can't run to the coffee shop because you saw what happened. Tomorrow there will be tourists hanging out there just to see if I stop by. The owner will get more business, but some people will be rude and not order drinks." She shook her head. "That's not what I wanted to say. I want to say that I like you a lot. I like your attitude, I like your smile, and I like having sex with you. Maybe we won't work out, but I want to try."

Daniel swallowed, then turned and set down his drink and the bag of food. He cupped her face gently, holding her still. "I wake up thinking about you. Sometimes it's sexual. Other times the dreams are just us hanging out. I want to be with you all the time. I know this will be difficult. I can't ask you to quit your job and hang out with me just like I'd resent you if you asked me to quit mine. I'll have to deploy next year, so that's six months in the sandbox."

She shook her head. "I'd never ask you to quit."

Daniel leaned his forehead against hers. "Can we do this? Have this crazy relationship?"

A smile played on her lips as happiness filled her. "Why not?" Her chest tightened, and her head spun. This could really be real. If Daniel could handle the pressure, maybe they could make it. She almost snorted out a laugh. The pressure got to her at times. She knew Daniel was strong, but there were times this life was more than she could manage. She had money, so she could get away, but Daniel had a job he couldn't run from.

She was thinking too much, spiraling about what

might happen and not giving them a chance. She had to calm down so they could work through this.

"I'd never cheat on you."

"I'll never cheat on you. But you can be assured there will be articles about me having a relationship with every co-star, whether they are male or female. It won't be true, but it will be out there."

He nodded. "I trust you."

"The film industry is tough on couples. It may look easy from the outside, but we have to have tough shells to get us through whatever they throw our way. Before meeting you, I promised myself I wouldn't date outside the film industry."

"Why me then?"

She held his gaze. "Because there's something almost magical that happens when you touch me. When we kiss, I feel like the world doesn't matter, only the two of us."

"Like this?" Daniel asked before he tilted his head and brushed his lips over hers.

"Mmm, yes."

"Or this?" Daniel swiped his tongue over the slit in her lips, and she opened, allowing him to explore. Her brain fizzed, and she tilted her head, giving him what he needed as she took from him. When he pulled back and met her gaze, he lifted his eyebrows like he had a question. She stared up at him in wonder, needing more of his kisses.

"So I take it that kiss was magical, too?"

"So magical," Rosalind whispered.

"What if I do this?"

Daniel ran his hands up her body and cupped her breasts before he squeezed. Then he pulled her shirt over her head. He paused and let his gaze wander.

"So beautiful."

"The bruises are almost gone."

His gaze met hers, and the fierceness almost made her take a step back. "I hate those bastards for hurting you."

"We survived."

He kissed her shoulder, then her neck, and made his way down to her breasts, kissing the tops of her mounds. He popped the front clasp and pushed her bra away before he looked up and met her gaze.

"You're okay with this?"

"I want you. I want all of you."

He groaned before he dipped his head and began the slow torture of bringing her to orgasm by just licking and sucking her nipples. She was desperate to come and was so close when he pulled away. His gaze crashed into hers as he pinched both nipples and tugged, making her gasp.

"So beautiful. I love seeing you orgasm."

He moved one hand between her legs and rubbed over her pants, putting just enough pressure to make her come. She cried out and gripped his shoulder with her good hand while the orgasm rolled over her.

When she could breathe again, he picked her up and

carried her to his bed, placing her gently in the center. He stripped off his clothes before he pulled off her shorts and panties, kissing her thighs, her hip, and then finally between her legs. He sucked her clit into his mouth, making her gasp. She was already sensitive and knew she wouldn't last, but that's how making love to Daniel was. He wanted to see her with her head thrown back, her mouth open as she gasped his name, and she wouldn't disappoint him.

By the time he slid into her, she'd come three times and was ready to come again. They were still using condoms, and she understood, but she wanted to feel his cum dripping down her leg because that meant they would be committed. The thought of it drove her to bliss, and she came again.

She wanted commitment with this man. Whatever she'd planned on having with Brock had seemed like a business deal compared to the raw passion she felt with Daniel. This was life.

Daniel pumped in and pulled out slowly, his gaze drilling into hers. "When I'm with you," he said as he slid in. "I'm complete." He pulled out and then slammed in, making her gasp.

His lips found hers, and he buried himself in her, torturing her with the slow grind of his hips that guaranteed her clit was being teased with each pump in. She was coming again as he rose up and pumped in fast, then stilled, his gasps echoing in the bedroom.

Instead of rolling off her, he kissed her cheek and

her neck, then brushed his lips over hers in a gentle slide. This man was power and tenderness wrapped up together.

"I like you a lot, Daniel Wilson."

He moved so he could stare into her eyes. He lifted off her, and she immediately missed the connection. "Rosalind Steel, I'm falling for you."

She gasped and sat up. "Oh dear, I never told you that's my stage name. My legal name is Rosalind Smejkal."

"Wait, what? Is that Russian?"

She laughed. "No, Czech. It's too hard to pronounce, so my first director told me to use something simple. He picked Steel."

"And it hasn't been leaked?"

"No one cares. I'm sure someone will try to make a big deal out of it at some point in the future, but not yet."

He shrugged. "It doesn't matter. You're the wonderful woman I'm falling for. Nothing will change that."

She couldn't believe her luck in finding this man. If she revealed their relationship, people would think they'd already been dating before Brock broke it off with her. No one would believe she was the innocent one in the relationship. They needed to talk about how to go about telling the world about them, but for now, she would just enjoy being with Daniel.

CHAPTER TWENTY-FIVE

*R*osalind lay sleeping in his bed, her hair spread out under her head. She looked like perfection, all cuddly and warm. She'd told him the night before she had a full day of reading scripts and planning but didn't need to be up early. A part of him wanted to wake her up with a kiss, but she needed the sleep. He could kiss her later.

Honestly, the last few weeks, other than the torture, had been the best in his life. He wasn't sure what to do when Rosalind packed up and headed to Canada. She had plans to come back after the movie was done filming, but that would be more than a month from today if they didn't have any production delays.

Dunk pulled in at the base, still sore from the torture he'd endured when he'd been captured. They'd survived, but he still had some issues.

"Hey, man, long time no see," Vine called out when he stepped from his SUV.

Dunk smiled and waved. "Good to see you."

"Are we still getting together on Friday?" Legs asked.

"Yes," Dunk said. "Rosalind leaves on Sunday morning. I want you all to meet her."

"Jesus, it's still odd to think about you dating her," Minx said.

"I know, but she really is a great person." Dunk had sent a text to the guys, telling them about Rosalind. No one was allowed to talk about her to anyone. They were reading the women in on the secret relationship this week, then introducing them to Rosalind on Friday. He prayed it went well because these guys were his buddies.

"Hey," Mustang called out across the parking lot.

Dunk waved as Mustang came over. "Good to see you."

"How are you feeling?" Mustang asked.

Dunk rolled his shoulders. "Still sore, but I'm good."

"I'm glad you're safe. Have you been released by the doctors yet?"

Dunk shook his head. "No, not for physical training. I'm hoping I'll get the go-ahead this week."

"Well, there's a shit storm brewing. I doubt your team will be sent in to fix their shit. There are two teams on ships in the Pacific who should go in. We'll need to test the plan for them, though."

Vine was beside them, walking into the building. "Sounds good. How has the last month been?"

Mustang threw his arm over Vine's shoulder. "Good. We missed you guys when we had obstacle course day. People on our team actually finished last. If you'd been here, you would have saved us the humiliation."

Vine threw back his head and laughed with Mustang. Dunk knew some guys didn't get along with other SEALs, but for the most part, everyone here in Hawaii were friends. The new class of SEALs was graduating soon, and they'd probably get a few new guys here for a while before they were placed on a team.

They stepped inside and didn't even have time to get coffee before they were called into the secure conference room. He texted Rosalind, telling her he would be unavailable all day.

Mustang had been correct. All hell had broken loose. The place was packed with twelve SEALs in the room, the officers, and a few other people. They were given a rundown of the situation and were expected to provide feedback. They had tapped into a few traffic cameras, so they had some eyes on the situation, but not nearly enough.

Dunk would rather be on the other side of this equation. He hated watching all the action play out when he could do nothing but offer suggestions. The guys on the ground didn't need some armchair quarterback running the show, and he guessed it was good that the Navy included people like him and the other SEALs in their conferences like this. At least they'd been in the field recently and had an idea of what would work, but sometimes even trained SEALs couldn't work out what was going on in the field, and the boots on the ground had to make it work.

By the time they stepped out of the room, it was almost time to go home. Their men had made it out. It had been close for a while, but all the SEALs had escaped. Two of the hostages had died, but the other four were okay. Dunk was glad he got to go home to Rosalind tonight. She made his life better.

After a quick meeting with Vine, they spent a little time cleaning before heading home. He wanted to take a quick shower and then spend the evening having sex, but when he got home, he noticed a sleek sports car on the street. His stomach tightened. He knew he had to share Rosalind with the world, but he didn't want to.

He opened the door to laughter. But it wasn't Rosalind's light and bubbly laughter. It was a guy. Jealousy whipped through him, but he pushed it away as he stepped in. She had said jealousy ended more relationships in Hollywood than actual offenses. He needed to remember that she was with him, and some random guy showing up at his house wasn't a threat.

He stepped into the den, and Rosalind jumped up and ran to him. Her hand was much better now, and she was using it, though she still didn't like physical therapy because they made her do stuff that hurt.

Two guys sitting at his table stood and moved closer. He might have recognized one of them from some movie poster he'd seen.

"Hi, I'm David, and this is my partner, Ben. I'm co-starring with Rosalind in the next movie."

Daniel kissed Rosalind on the top of the head and wrapped one arm around her before sticking out his hand to shake hands.

"It's nice to meet you, David and Ben."

"Thank you," Ben said. "Sorry for intruding. We flew out here when Rosalind said she was in Hawaii. We wanted to meet you."

"Oh," he blinked at Ben, then turned to Rosalind, unsure he understood.

"Dating someone in the film industry can be difficult," Ben said. "I've been with David for two years, but we haven't gone public yet."

David shrugged. "We just don't do any kissing or holding hands in public."

"It's my choice," Ben said. "I'm the one not wanting to go public. People still think David is straight—"

"I'm bi, not straight," David said.

Ben shrugged. "It's just part of fame. People develop this fantasy in their heads about movie stars. I can guarantee that some article will be written about how Rosalind was seen coming from David's room at four in the morning or vice versa. If it's true, it's because they finished filming at three, and Rosalind had extra makeup remover, a sleeping pill, or something else. They aren't having an affair."

Dunk grunted, unsure how to respond. Rosalind lifted on her toes and kissed his jaw. He hadn't been expecting these guys to be here, and the subject had been weighing on his mind. He knew that just because David was dating Ben didn't mean he wouldn't sleep with someone.

"Sorry, I'm a little tired, and this is…"

Ben reached out and squeezed his biceps. "Jesus." Ben shook his head. "Sorry, I don't mean to man-handle you. Before I got distracted by your muscles, I was going to say that dating in this business requires trust. I trust David."

"And I trust Ben," David said. "If you stay with Rosalind, I'm sure you'll go through some rough patches, and the first article will probably piss you off, but you have to trust each other."

"I'll keep that in mind." Dunk glanced down, finding Rosalind staring up at him. Her gaze was filled with love and devotion. The look made his breath catch. She was beautiful, but it was more than beauty. She cared for him, and he cared deeply for her.

"We should get out of your hair," Ben said.

Dunk ripped his gaze away from Rosalind's. "How about you stay for dinner? I'm grilling steaks."

"Are you sure we won't be in the way?" David asked.

"I'd love to have you stay," Dunk said. And he wasn't

just saying that. This man would be a part of Rosalind's life for the next few weeks. And then he guessed when the movie came out, she and David would have to travel together to do promotions. He would be nice and make friends because he was expecting the same from Rosalind and his friends.

They spent the evening laughing and talking. David was surprised that Dunk hadn't seen any of his movies. Dunk thought it made things easier because if he was the type of guy who had seen all the movies, he had little doubt he would be awestruck.

At around eight, the guys left after helping him wash dishes and clean the kitchen. Rosalind gave him a tight hug after they'd shut the door.

"What is that for?" Dunk asked.

"You were great with David and Ben. Thank you. Next week we'll be on set together, spending all day talking between takes. I'm glad he met you, and we can talk openly about our relationships. It makes it easier."

Dunk nodded. "Ben is nice."

"He's a good guy. We've met before. He honestly wasn't going to stay with David, but they worked it out and decided that the crap they would have to deal with was worth it."

He turned to face her, taking in the serious look on her face. The emotions flowing through him were thick. "Do you think we're worth it?"

"I do. I really do. I don't want to rush this, but

Daniel, I've fallen for you. We've kind of discussed it in a roundabout way, but we haven't said the words."

"I love you," Dunk said before Rosalind could say more.

Laughter spilled out and washed over him. "I love you, too."

Her lips were plastered against his, showing him how she felt. She stripped off his pants and underwear while he took off his shirt. She was on her knees, sucking and licking him, driving him crazy. He needed to get her on her back, but she had other plans as she pushed him into a kitchen chair and then straddled him, sinking down slowly on his cock.

"Oh damn, that feels good," Dunk moaned as she rose and sank down on his cock again.

Her slow movements were satisfying as hell and drove him crazy. This woman was much more than he deserved, and he loved her deeply. He would miss her like crazy when she was gone, but when they were together, he'd find heaven.

CHAPTER TWENTY-SIX

*R*osalind's palms were damp when they pulled up at Vine's house. She could face down a room full of reporters, but meeting Daniel's friends had her on edge.

"They'll love you." Daniel squeezed her hand.

"They've seen movies I've been in, read rumor reports, heard me give pithy interviews, and they've probably already reached conclusions on me. I don't know that they'll love me."

"Babe, you're just like everyone else in there. They aren't going to judge you."

Rosalind leaned over and kissed Daniel, knowing he didn't get her fear. She had anxiety about this and hadn't slept well the night before. While Daniel had been at work, she'd spent the day reading the same line repeatedly, not moving forward at all.

"Come on, let's go."

Daniel hopped out and raced around to get the door for her. They weren't holding hands in public because he'd agreed that they should keep their relationship secret for a while. If their relationship survived, it would be easier to reveal their status than to protect Daniel if the press knew and they'd broken up.

The door opened when they were only halfway up the walk. Her stomach pitched as she spied the room full of people just beyond the man standing in the doorway. A woman stepped out and moved toward her.

"Hi, I'm Jenna. We're an overwhelming crew, but I swear I've told them they have to be on their best behavior."

A tiny girl ran out from behind the man and dashed toward them. She paused when she got to their feet and stared up at Rosalind. She'd done one live-action children's film and guessed this little girl had seen it.

"Wow! But where is your hair?" the tiny girl asked.

Rosalind squatted down to be at eye level with the child and smiled. "It's blonde now, not red."

"How'd that happen?" the child asked.

"I wore a wig when I was in that movie."

"A wig?" The girl looked up at her mother, who picked her up. "Mommy was right. It was a wig."

Jenna chuckled as Rosalind stood, a little less nervous since there were kids here. She had almost felt like she was walking into an ambush, but the child had calmed her nerves. Funny how a child could cut through the crap and make her feel good about the situation.

Daniel led her inside, and she was introduced to everyone. There were so many people, but one of them had been nice and made nametags. After an hour of mingling and talking with them, she felt like these people were her friends. They were all nice, and none of them made a big deal out of her being an actress. They didn't ask who she knew or any awkward questions. Instead, they treated her like one of their gang. She liked that.

On the way home, Daniel glanced over and smiled. "You like them?"

She nodded. "They're good people. I was worried before we got there."

"I'm glad you have all of their numbers now. If we get sent out on a mission, one of them will send you a text."

"It must be strange having such a stressful job."

He shrugged. "It's normal for me. It's just what I do."

"Were you cleared by the medical team?"

A frown turned down the corners of his mouth. "Not yet. I'm being antsy, and they said it will take time. I guess I just need to take it easy and heal more."

"Well, we can take it easy tonight and just hang out."

"Sounds good." He reached over and took her hand, squeezing twice.

They didn't do much on Saturday other than having

sex. On Sunday morning, when Rosalind's alarm rang, sadness hit hard. She didn't want to go, and by the way he clung to her, she knew he felt it, too.

"Hey," Daniel said after a long moment of them hugging.

"Hey yourself."

"I know you have commitments. This is one of them. We're going to be okay when you leave."

She nodded, wishing they had more time. "I'm going to miss you."

"I'll miss you. If the Navy called me up right now, I'd go. Your job is calling you, and now you get to leave. I'll see you when you get back." He sounded so calm about everything, and she just wanted to throw a fit. But he was right, this was a part of her job, and she needed to get on the plane and fly to Vancouver.

She brushed her lips over his, her heart squeezing hard. She'd hired a car to get her to the airport. Though he wanted to drop her off and say goodbye, they agreed it wouldn't be fair for Daniel to be introduced to the world when she was leaving for more than a month. Later, they would have the time to share the good news of their relationship.

The car drove away, and she felt like her heart was ripping from her chest. Leaving had never been hard like this. It was like she'd left a part of herself behind.

CHAPTER TWENTY-SEVEN

*D*aniel sat in the doctor's office, waiting for results. He figured today was the day he'd get the all-clear to start back with the team. He'd been going into work, doing paper shuffling, filling roles for people who called in sick, doing some analysis for other teams, working on back-end stuff, but not doing the hard physical training the SEALs were doing. If his team was called in for action, he wouldn't go. A part of him feared they would replace him with one of the new guys. There were five guys on base who weren't attached to teams. One of them could easily step in and fill his position. A few guys he knew were retiring, but there were more SEALs than positions on established teams open.

The door opened, and the doctor stepped in, his smile wide. "Daniel, it's good to see you."

He and the doctor had dispensed with the ranks on

181

their last appointment. It was a little odd, but he would get used to it.

"So, Doc, can you give me the all-clear? I'm ready to get back to the action."

"Actually, son, no."

"What?" Panic raced through him. What was he going to do? Being a SEAL was his life now.

"Don't react yet. Hear me out."

He didn't want to cry, but tears were close to the surface. What would he have to live for if he wasn't a SEAL? "Okay. I don't like the sound of it, though."

"You need more time to heal. Your internal injuries were extensive. The concussion you got was too much to heal in this short time. If you go out on a mission and have anything happen, you're out of teams for good. You can train, as long as there are no smoke grenades, flashbangs, nothing concussive, no jumping out of planes, no dropping huge distances. You can lift weights, do some biking—"

Anger whipped through him as the disappointment rose. "So workout in a gym."

"Daniel, it's a start. This is a path back to get onto the teams. If I released you to jump back in and your body failed on a mission, there's more to think about than just you. Your teammates could be hurt, too. The teams are only as strong as their weakest man. You aren't strong enough to be the threat you need to be. Give it three months to get back into fighting shape, and I'll most likely release you."

He closed his eyes and fought the emotions. He felt the doctor move close, and the pad of the table he was sitting on dipped. Doc's arm came around his shoulder.

"This is a wake-up call. You should figure out what you want to do besides being a SEAL. The decision doesn't have to be made now, but Daniel, loads of guys get medicaled out. If you are injured again, the Navy would be irresponsible to allow you to stay in the SEAL program."

"Fuck, Doc, this is the worst news."

"No, I just gave the worst news to a young ensign just before I came in here. She has breast cancer that has spread to her brain. She's got maybe three months to live, and her daughter is only two years old. You have inconvenient news that will make you change how you're living, maybe. Heal, enjoy life, and live it to the fullest. If that's being on a SEAL team, then that's what it is. If it's changing your job in the Navy to serve in another way, then great, but live because right now there are probably a few hundred US citizens and military personnel learning today they won't see their next birthday."

Daniel watched the door close, feeling like the doctor had just kicked him in the balls. He hopped off the table and straightened his clothes before heading into the hall. The doc's words echoed in his mind as he headed to base.

Doc was right. He could live. He wanted to choose life. Being with Rosalind had opened his eyes to how good things could be. Once he was out of the SEALs, he wanted to spend more time with her. Maybe his life didn't have to be about teams and going on missions. He loved his job, loved taking down bad guys and showing them who was boss, but there were more jobs in the military than just being on teams. Thousands of people supported the SEALs, and he always respected the guys who'd been SEALs before switching to support roles. They knew what it took and knew what they were going through.

"Hey, Dunk, how'd it go?" Quirk called out as he stepped into the room.

Dunk wiped his hand over his face, wanting to be positive for these men. The truth was either death or medical reasons would pull these guys from the teams, and he sure as hell hoped they'd be sixty-year-old men playing golf together or sitting around shooting the shit instead of being six feet under.

"I'm not cleared for missions, but I can start working out again."

"Oh shit," Minx said. "That sucks."

Dunk shook his head. "No, it really doesn't. I'm alive, and I have a chance to live more days. I don't want to give up being a SEAL, but we all know our time on teams is limited."

The guys were all standing close now. Astro reached out and squeezed his shoulder. He didn't want to be a downer, but the doc's words had resonated inside.

"Being a SEAL is a dream come true. I will work hard to get back onto the teams, but if I have to move to a different role, that's what I'll do. I'd rather we all be sitting around a campfire in twenty years, shooting the shit with each other, than talking about how sad your kids were at your funeral."

"Damn, Dunk. That's depressing," Astro said.

He nodded. "Doc put me in my place. There was a young ensign in the office before me who won't live more than three months."

"What?" Wig asked.

"She has cancer. Me having to work my way back onto the teams isn't the worst news out there. I'm okay. If I don't make it back to mission ready, I'll find a new passion and move forward, but that ensign, she has a baby, and now she's going to die. That kid won't know why. I want to live fully, not some half-life where I'm miserable because of some circumstance that knocked me out of teams. I can live with whatever happens because I know I was a damn good SEAL and did all I could to make our missions successful. If I'm not ready to go out, I sure as shit don't want to put you guys at risk."

Vine pulled him in for a hug. "Dude, that's the most impressive thing I've ever heard anyone say. Thank you for not being a jerk about this."

"Man, it's tough. I wanted to throw a fit, but the doc was right. I'm still here. There are so many who don't make it back."

"Truth," Minx said.

They all hugged him, messing up his hair or slapping him on the back. When he'd come here and joined this team, he didn't know if he would fit in, but these guys were his brothers. He loved them like family.

He gave Vine the list of things the doctor had restricted him from doing. It wasn't a huge list, but it would change a few things they did. They dressed in their shorts and headed out for a short run and then a weightlifting session.

That night when Rosalind called, he listened to her day and chatted about his, not telling her he'd been depressed about the doctor's decision. Because, in reality, he had more to live for than he'd thought. He was in love with Rosalind and wanted to see where life took them.

"You're rather quiet," Rosalind said.

He chuckled. "I miss you. There's more to life than just being a Navy SEAL."

"Yeah, like what?" she asked.

"Being your man, holding you close at night, being with you when we travel."

"Those seem like life plans," Rosalind said.

"They are, but I'm not going to go into details while you're in Alaska. I'm glad the movie is going well, and you've had good days of filming. I hope the weather stays good."

"Same. We're doing three more days here then heading to Vancouver to film inside."

"Have fun your last few days in Alaska. Tell David and Ben I said hello."

"Will do. And Daniel."

"Yeah, babe?"

"I love you. I'll see you in a few weeks."

"I love you. Stay safe."

He ended the call, happy he'd had a chance to talk to her. She'd been working until midnight for a few days, so she hadn't called. It was great talking to her, but he wanted her in his arms again. Waking up to sexy dreams about her and then realizing she wasn't in bed with him had been like a knife to his heart, but she would be back with him soon.

CHAPTER TWENTY-EIGHT

*E*xcitement mixed with worry as the plane landed in Honolulu. Rosalind hadn't spoken with Daniel on the phone for five days. She'd texted that she was flying out as soon as possible, but she hadn't dropped the exact date and time until right before the plane took off.

She turned on her phone, waiting for it to connect as the plane taxied. The flight hadn't been bad, and she'd gotten on last minute so people on the plane had no idea she was on this flight, and she would get off first since she was in the first row. It amazed her how easy it was for her to travel if she wore large glasses and a ball cap.

Her phone buzzed in her hand, and she glanced at the screen, seeing a barrage of texts from Daniel. She pulled up the application to read the texts, and her lips spread into a huge smile. He was at the airport in baggage claim waiting for her. Her heart expanded, and she felt tears prick her eyes. She was traveling light because she wanted to go shopping here and buy a wardrobe for Hawaii. She also needed to buy a place, maybe a condo somewhere behind a gate or in a high-rise with security. If they were going to be here for Daniel's job, they needed protection.

Daniel might be a badass SEAL, but she wasn't and didn't enjoy sleeping in a place that didn't have a security guard looking after the area. It wasn't anything she'd discussed with the team on-set, but at night, she'd had to resort to blocking her door with chairs and setting up glasses with silverware in the doorway to make noise if anyone entered while she slept. She needed the comfort of having security.

Luckily, no one recognized her as she made her way off the plane and into the terminal. She had a good disguise for now but knew it wouldn't work forever. She'd texted Daniel what she was wearing and that they needed to move to a private area to kiss once she exited the secure area.

She spied him first and then saw the smile spread over his face. He lifted his chin, and excitement filled her. When she got close, he took her bag but not her hand as they moved through the terminal.

She drew in a deep breath and sighed. "I love being here."

He glanced at her and smiled. "I love you."

His words made her skin tingle. She couldn't wait

to get to his place and do all the things she'd fantasized doing with him.

They were beside his SUV, and he paused to glance around before he moved them between the vehicles and brushed his lips over hers. She closed her eyes and leaned in against him.

"I missed you," Rosalind said.

"I went grocery shopping so we have food at home."

"Good, because once we get there, I don't want to leave."

The sounds of people talking made them break apart, and he held the door open for her. She stepped in and sighed as he shut the door. She could relax now.

The drive to his place wasn't long. When they arrived, they went straight inside, and he caught her before she got too far.

"I need to shower. I feel gross."

"Let's shower together, and I'll wash your hair. I got good at it when you were here before."

Her eyes burned with tears. "I missed you so much."

His lips curved up in a smile. "Come on. Shower and bed, maybe some food."

"Yes, for some food."

She brushed her teeth first, then Daniel moved in close, kissing her as he helped her out of her clothes. It felt right being with Daniel. She didn't know how life would play out, but she wanted to make this work with him.

He stepped them into the shower, and she let him

rub soap all over her body, finding all her sensitive spots. She gasped as he slid his hands around to her ass and pulled her close, sliding his cock between them. She wanted to feel him deep inside her, but she didn't want to rush this.

After he washed and conditioned her hair, he washed off and then pinned her against the wall as he brought her to the first of her orgasms. He shut off the water and helped her dry before carrying her to the bed. He had a plan, and she was along for the ride.

His tongue did wicked things to her, swiping over her pussy like he knew her inside out. He teased another orgasm out of her, then moved to her breasts, knowing she loved him to play with her nipples.

When she was about to come again, he rolled on a condom and slid in as her next orgasm hit. His lips trailed over her neck to her ear before finding her mouth. He made love to her like no one else ever had.

She had her legs wrapped around his hips, and his arms were braced beside her head as he pumped into her. Their gazes locked. Their love for each other was so evident that it made her want to explode with happiness.

He shoved in hard and stilled before he dropped low, his lips pressing against hers as he jerked and gasped. When he pulled out, he wrapped his arms around her, holding her close. The emotions they shared were near earth-shattering. She couldn't imagine life without him.

"I'm so glad you're here now," Daniel said.

"I need to buy a place here."

Daniel jerked back, his eyes narrowed. "Why?"

She blew out a breath, knowing she'd broached the subject in the wrong way. "Babe, I can't—wait, that's not how I wanted to talk about this."

His lips thinned, and she smoothed her hand over his cheek. "It's not bad. Let's get up and get some food, and I can explain."

He nodded, but she worried he was already making up reasons to pull away from her. She didn't know if she could express everything correctly and not piss him off.

CHAPTER TWENTY-NINE

*D*unk pulled out the lunch meat, trying not to be angry at Rosalind for suggesting she didn't want to stay with him when she came to Hawaii. He shouldn't jump to conclusions, but he didn't like that she was talking about getting her own place right after they'd had sex.

She moved beside him and glanced up, worry filling her eyes. He hated that look on her face and wanted to smooth the fear away, but what if she didn't want him to?

"Okay, so while I was away filming, some stuff happened."

His heart nearly shattered. Was this her way of breaking up with him?

"What happened?" he asked, trying not to sound angry.

"We didn't always sleep in the hotels. We had

trailers for those nights we had late filming then had to be back on set early the next morning." Rosalind shivered as she reached for a plate. A new type of worry hit him, and he wondered if something had happened to her.

"Did someone hurt you?"

She shook her head. "No, it was all in my mind. I couldn't sleep unless I knew a security guard was watching. It got worse for a while. I was blocking the door with glasses set up with silverware in them. I just need someplace with a security guard, especially if you get called out on a mission while I'm here."

He blinked at her, trying to realign his thinking. She wasn't breaking it off. She was making a permanent home here. She plowed forward, talking so fast he couldn't interrupt her.

"I just want a place, maybe a condo with a security guard or a gated community to live in. And I don't expect you to pay for the house. I have the money, and it's silly, but I'm too scared to sleep at night if I don't have someone there with me, guarding the door."

He lifted his hand and placed a finger on her mouth, getting her to stop talking. "So you want me to move in with you?"

"I know this may be weird. I just—" She met his gaze, sadness filling her eyes.

The look took his breath away. He pulled her into a hug and didn't let go for a long moment.

"Babe, I'm sorry you're experiencing so much fear. I want you to feel safe."

"Would you consider moving in with me?" Rosalind asked.

"What if you decide you don't like me anymore?"

"I'm not going to kick you out if that's what you're worried about."

"Won't it cost a lot to maintain a house here?"

She shook her head. "Not really."

"What if I get moved to California or Virginia?"

She shrugged. "Then I guess we'll live there."

"But what about the house here?"

She lifted her eyebrows. "Wouldn't it be nice to have a place to stay if we visit?"

"Wait, you're willing to drop a few hundred thousand on a place you won't be at all the time?"

She turned and cupped his cheeks, getting him to turn to face her. "It will be more than a few hundred thousand, and yes. I want to feel safe, and I know a part of that can be helped with therapy which I haven't gotten and need to see someone about, but a part of it is the reality that once someone knows I'm here in this house living with you, this place will become a target. People will block the streets, and while I don't mind this place, I actually like it. It feels like home. The neighbors will hate us once tourists start looking for this house."

That worried him. He couldn't have people hanging

out here, getting into everyone's business. "Do you really think they will?"

"You saw what happened to the coffee shop. They had photos of people camped out there for days."

He nodded slowly. "They did have some problems. They made a lot of money, but they had to use some of that money to replace the chairs and tables out front when someone stole them."

Shock filled her. "What? I had no idea. Oh no, I feel terrible."

"Don't. I heard the owner talking, and they've made back much more than the thieves took."

"That sucks. People just can't be nice anymore. So can you imagine people trying to look in through the curtains or breaking in just to get a photo of me?"

"Damn, that would be bad. I can't have that here in this neighborhood."

"No, it's not a big enough place for that type of shenanigans. I don't want you to be in danger either. It's not like a mission where you can eliminate the bad guys. These people will have their cameras out filming everything. Even if you are doing everything right, you could end up in trouble if someone takes offense to your actions. What if you needed to get to the base, and some people decided to block you? If you inched through the crowd, someone would claim you hit them, even if you didn't."

He ran his hand over his stubble, then tugged on his chin as he dropped his head back and stared up at the ceiling. "It would be an asshole move to tell you no. So I'm not doing that. But I feel like I'd be living off you."

She put her hand on the back of his head, encouraging him to look at her. He was struck by her beauty. It wasn't just how she looked but how she made him feel that made her even more beautiful than any other woman he'd ever seen.

"You would offer me a place to stay without asking for a dime if I had no money."

He nodded. "That's true."

"I'm not saying I'll pay for everything, but I can't stay here long-term. It wouldn't be safe for either of us or your neighbors. In time this street will be crawling with people wanting to get a look, and some people will take it too far. Your neighbors will be pissed if they have to fight through crowds just to get to the grocery store."

"I can't have you stay here if I get called out."

She shook her head. "It would be too dangerous. How about we find a place that will offer the security I need and not be somewhere you'd feel awkward living."

His eyes narrowed. "Awkward?"

She chuckled. "There's this condo in Waikiki that is amazing. It's over the top. Like Elton John owns the penthouse. There is also a dress requirement in the elevator and the lobby. I don't think you coming home in your workout apparel would be okay with some of the residents."

"Oh, no. I can't live in a place with a dress require-ment for the elevator."

"No, that would be unseemly. I'll contact a discreet agent who will set us up with a nice place where we will both be happy."

He blew out a breath, letting go of the ego he wanted to desperately hold on to. "Okay, I agree. But you have to go see someone about the PTSD."

She nodded, and relief spread through him. He was addicted to her kisses so he leaned in and brushed his lips over hers. She heaved a sigh as she curled her fingers around his waist.

"We need to eat," he whispered.

"I know." She stepped back, and he wanted her close again.

This thing between them was growing in a way he wasn't really prepared for. He thought he knew what it felt like to have a girlfriend, but with Rosalind, every-thing was more. He wanted to live with her and spend his free time with her, but their lives were so different. They would need a deep bond to get through everything.

CHAPTER THIRTY

"*H*ey, man," Vine called out as Dunk headed to the parking lot.

He turned back and waved. "Hey."

"We thought we would celebrate your return to the team this weekend."

Dunk smiled. "Heck yeah. I'm excited."

"It's good you're better. It sucks that you were out. How did today feel?"

"Good." They'd spent the morning shooting, then the afternoon breaching buildings. He was sore, but not in a bad way.

"Jenna will be happy to see Rosalind again."

"Yeah, she's happy to be back."

"Have you two done anything other than lay in bed?"

Dunk chuckled. "We've been to the beach once."

"One time! I'm surprised you put clothes on and went out in public."

Thoughts of Rosalind naked and in his arms made him heat. He pushed aside the erotic musings. "We've been looking at houses."

"Wait, why?" Vine asked.

"She thinks it could be dangerous not being behind a gate. I don't know. Maybe it will be, but maybe it won't."

"Safety is important. You have to take care of your family. Look at Quirk and Carbon. They have to live in a gated community."

He shrugged. "I haven't thought about it that way."

"We support you no matter where you live."

After shooting the shit with the guys for a bit, he headed home. He wasn't really convinced they needed to move to a gated community. He wasn't going to push back, though. He stepped in, happy to see Rosalind sitting at the kitchen table, going through a script.

"How was your day?" Dunk asked.

"I paid the coffee shop a visit and took a few photos with an iced coffee and their logo on full display. The owner appreciated the free advertising. We talked, and she doesn't blame me for the vandalism."

"That's good. I'm glad you feel better about that."

"I do. I also set up the shoe auction with six other actresses. We weren't going to include the men, but I spoke with a few, and they have some stuff they'd like to donate. The money will go to a homeless shelter in LA, an LGBT community center, and a youth activities center that needs new sports equipment."

"Wow, that's awesome. It sounds like you've had a productive day. So how is the script you're reading? Is it any good?"

She rolled her eyes. "This one, no. I'm going to pass. I just want to see what the ending says."

He nodded, but still didn't understand what made her think a script was worth taking. He'd read a little bit of one she turned down and he thought it was good. But she was the expert and knew what she liked. "Ah. I'm going to shower."

She glanced up, a wicked smile spreading over her face. "I'll join you in a moment."

He really liked when she joined him. He knew part of it was their relationship was new, but he hoped they never lost this fire.

The cool water felt good on his back. Rosalind stepped in after he finished washing his hair and grabbed the soap, spreading it over his back and between his butt cheeks. He chuckled and knew he would return the favor.

He rinsed off and was about to push her under the spray when he heard an odd noise. He met Rosalind's gaze and lifted his finger to his mouth, telling her to be quiet. He heard the noise again, and panic raced through him.

"Get down low, sit in the bottom of the tub, and don't move."

Rosalind's eyes went wide, and she nodded before dropping low. He grabbed a towel, stepped out, and wrapped the material around his waist. He glanced back to make sure Rosalind was still in the tub. The shower curtain had closed so he couldn't see her, which was best. He didn't want anyone to see her.

He moved to the window, intent on looking out the sliver of a view at the side of the curtain. He leaned over, holding his breath so he didn't move the material. He expected to see the bushes and grass. Instead, he saw a full-grown man with a fucking huge camera lens pointed at him. Anger whipped through him, and he pushed open the curtain and then unlocked the window.

"What the fuck are you doing in my yard?"

He could hear the camera clicking. Great, the bastard was taking his photo through the screen.

"Is she in there with you? Just a shot. We just want one shot. I'll give you a million for a shot of her."

The blood drained from his head as reality sank in. Rosalind was in danger because she was in his tiny house without protection.

Dunk slammed the window closed and pulled the curtains so no one could see in. He moved to the shower and noticed his hands were shaking. He glanced in and saw tears filling Rosalind's eyes.

"Holy shit. I'm so sorry. I should have moved us out

the moment you came home. Fuck, Rosalind, I fucked up. I'm sorry."

She held out her hand, and he stepped into the shower, not caring that the water was still running and the towel would be soaked. He pulled her up and held her close as she wrapped her arms around him.

"It's not your fault. It's them. They do this, not you. We can get a room at one of the hotels with good security."

"Shit. I need to get you out of here. This sucks. I'm so sorry."

The sound of sirens filled his little house, and he knew he had to get Rosalind in clothes, or they would have more than just some horrible photographer seeing her.

"Clothes," Dunk said.

Rosalind nodded and moved to step from the shower, but he stopped her.

"Just a sec. Let me get you a towel."

She shut the water off as he dropped his soaked towel and then moved to grab her a dry towel. She'd dried, and they were pulling on their clothes when his doorbell rang. He met her gaze and nodded.

"I'll see if I can get them to leave," Dunk said.

"Thank you." Rosalind settled on his bed before he closed the door. She had warned him it would get worse. For some reason, he'd thought they could get away with living here for a while longer.

He pulled open the front door, finding the cops

with three guys standing next to them in cuffs. "Excuse me, sir. These guys say they know you. That you wanted them here on your property."

He shook his head. "I've never met them. They're here to harass me."

The cops turned to look at the men. "I think you'll find they are photographers who sell images to magazines or online sites."

"You mean like those papazzies?" the tallest officer asked.

"Paparazzi, you dope," another officer said.

"Why would they be here at your place?"

"I have no clue," Dunk said. He hoped the lie didn't come back and bite him in the ass.

"She's in there!" one of the photographers with black frizzy hair yelled.

Dunk shrugged. "Listen, I don't know what he's talking about."

The officers rolled their eyes. "We're taking you three in for trespassing."

"We have rights," the frizzy-haired guy said as the officers led them down the walkway to the street.

Dunk stood in the doorway until the officers had the guys in the back of their cars. Once the police drove away, Dunk shut the door and moved to the bedroom, where he found Rosalind packing his bag. She glanced up and shook her head.

"Thank you. I have a room booked in a hotel with a kitchenette. It's in Waikiki, so your travel time may differ to the base. We have an appointment to look at a house this afternoon. I think this is the one. It's not too over the top, but it looks secure."

"Sounds good. I'll check and make sure I have everything I need for in the morning. I'll come back after my shift at the base and grab anything else I need."

She moved to him and cupped his cheeks. "Thank you."

"Hey, your safety is more important than living here. I've been happy with this house, but I don't want to put you at risk."

"I'll make it up to you."

He grabbed her by the shoulders and held her still. "You owe me nothing."

She searched his eyes, then nodded. "Okay, but I promise it won't always be this hectic."

"I know."

They headed to the hotel, which was one of those posh places he'd never been into. Rosalind directed him to a service elevator at the back corner of the garage. Sure enough, a woman in a dark suit was waiting for them with a dozen white roses.

"Hello, Miss Steel. Thank you for choosing us. My name is Flora Jackson. We have your room ready and used your dossier on file. Is that okay?"

"Yes. This is Mr. Wilson. He will be staying with me. Please make sure your staff knows that he is with me."

"Yes, Miss Steel. Right this way."

They rode the employee elevator up to the top

floor, none of them speaking. Rosalind looked very boss, like one of the women on base, focused and intense. The elevator opened to a gray hall and then they were led into an opulent space that he could tell was over the top.

"This floor is for our exclusive guests only. There are four other rooms up here, and two are currently occupied. If you need to go out but don't want to be seen, just call downstairs, and someone will meet you at the service elevator to take you down. The bar is open for another thirty minutes, and the kitchen can cook anything you need."

"Thank you, Flora. You've been a great help. I really appreciate it."

Flora opened the door, and Dunk almost choked on how beautiful the room was. Flora opened the blinds and flashed an apologetic smile.

"Of course, in the morning the view is more stunning. You can see the lights of Waikiki and Diamond Head now, but trust me, it will be a beautiful view tomorrow. If you need anything at all, please don't hesitate to ask."

Flora left, and Dunk turned around slowly, taking in the crystal chandelier, the overstuffed couches, and the vase in the center of the table where Flora had put the white roses.

"I can say with one hundred percent certainty I've never slept in a hotel room like this."

Rosalind smiled and moved closer. "Just wait until you see the shower."

"Oh, really?" He touched her hair. "We didn't get a chance to wash your hair. Maybe we should try it out."

A wicked grin spread over her face. "Let's get naked and see what happens."

Before they left the main room, Dunk closed the curtains, ensuring no one could see in. The last thing he wanted was photos of them together spreading over the internet. It was bad enough that people had shown up at his place to get pictures of Rosalind. From now on, he would use his skills to protect her from prying eyes. When she was in Hawaii, she would be safe.

CHAPTER THIRTY-ONE

*T*hey found a perfect house with just enough security to satisfy them both and an amazing back yard with so many flowers and plants it felt like they were in paradise. Daniel even admitted he really liked the place. The pool was an added benefit he enjoyed.

They planned to have his friends over on Sunday to celebrate. They'd gotten together a few times over the month they lived in the hotel, but this was the first time the crew had seen their new house. Rosalind was a little self-conscious about the place. It was beautiful but a little over the top, and it was large with four bedrooms and five baths, including the bungalow at the pool.

"You ready?" Daniel asked as the first of the cars pulled up.

"As ready as I'll ever be," Rosalind said.

"They love you, don't doubt that."

She blew out a breath, hoping he was right. Money made people do silly stuff at times. She didn't want this group to hate her because she could afford nice things.

The rest of the group arrived before Jenna and Vine could get inside. They headed inside, and before they could get to the kitchen, the guys were already asking for a tour. She laughed because she'd thought the women would ask first, but Daniel had been right. The men wanted to see the place.

"Don't forget to show them your security closet," Rosalind said.

"Oh yeah, you guys are going to love that." Daniel waved the guys to follow.

She'd been impressed with the camera system he'd set up, making sure they had full coverage of the entire lot. The house also came with a panic room, which she didn't think she would need, but was glad it was there.

"I want to see the closets," Sunshine said.

Jenna raised her hand. "The bathroom is what I want to take a look at."

"I just want to see it all," Audrey said.

They all laughed, and Rosalind began the tour. The kids enjoyed going around looking at the place, but they were ready to head outside to the pool by the end of the tour.

The kids had a great time, and Rosalind enjoyed hanging out with the adults. It was much more relaxed than parties with Hollywood types.

"So when are you filming next?" Audrey asked.

"I fly out on Tuesday."

"Ugh, don't remind me," Dunk said.

"If we got called up to go, you'd be in your truck headed to base in minutes," Wig said.

Daniel nodded as he moved behind her and placed his hands on her shoulders. "I know. I'm just going to miss you so much." He kissed the top of her head.

She looked up at him, and her heart jumped. She would miss her guy. He was so much more than someone to have sex with or fill her time. Daniel was a true partner. She wished they were alone, but they would have time to make love later.

"So, what are you working on?" Jenna asked.

"It's a secret." She pinched her forefinger and thumb together and made a zipper motion.

"Have you told Dunk?" Astro asked.

She shook her head. "I signed a non-disclosure agreement. I can't tell anyone. Not even people I know are on the project. They're bringing me in to film something else, too. That I can talk about. It's a comedy."

"Who is the co-star?"

Rosalind squeezed Daniel's hand. They'd talked about her starring opposite this actor, and he admitted he was jealous. But he had nothing to worry about.

"That smile. Oh my, who is it?" Sunshine begged.

"It's Ryan Reynolds," Rosalind said.

"What?!" all the women shouted, and the kids stopped playing to stare at them.

Rosalind laughed and answered the questions she could, leaving some details out. Daniel's friends were great. They were happy for her and weren't trying to get something from her. None of them had once taken a photo and posted it on social media. She didn't think any of them had taken her picture. They weren't bragging that she was their friend. Instead, they all took it in stride that they hung out together.

They had a great time with the gang. She enjoyed spending time with the guys Daniel worked with and their significant others. Close to five their friends took off. Daniel shut the door, then turned and hit her with a sexy stare. She knew what that look meant, and she took off, running to the bedroom, pulling off her shirt along the way.

Daniel's laughter trailed behind her. She loved this man. They needed more time, but she knew they would have a good life if they stayed together.

CHAPTER THIRTY-TWO

*D*unk had said goodbye to Rosalind, trying not to let the sadness show. How in the world did the people who loved military men and women do this? Rosalind was going off to film, and she wouldn't be in danger, but he felt like he would die if something happened to her. He didn't think he could trade positions with her.

On Friday morning, his phone rang before his alarm, and excitement pinged through him at the prospect of talking to Rosalind. But it wasn't Rosalind's name on the screen. Instead, it was his sister, Dianna. He hadn't heard from her in a few weeks, and he should have been more worried, but he'd let it slide since he'd been dealing with moving, his health issues, safety for Rosalind, and work.

"Dianna, how are you?"

"I have your girlfriend."

The voice wasn't Dianna, and Dunk froze. His heart may have jerked to a stop before racing hard. Lyle had been bad news, and he should have done more to investigate the jerk before Dianna became so involved with him.

"What are you going to do?" Dunk kept his voice even, trying not to reveal the panic racing through him. He stood from the bed, knowing he had to get moving.

"You're going to fly here, and I'll show you just what you made me lose when you were dumb enough to be captured by that gang."

He wanted to argue with the man but didn't want Rosalind hurt. She'd already suffered so much. She said the finger thing didn't bother her, but he knew it did since she hadn't revealed the loss to the press yet.

"Don't hurt her or Dianna."

Lyle let out a bark of a laugh. "Just get here, now."

"Where are you?"

"I'm texting you the location."

The line went dead. It only took him seconds to copy the information and send it to Vine with an explanation that Rosalind had been abducted by his sister's worthless ex.

Lyle was holding Rosalind hostage in her own house in Hollywood. She had to be scared. Shit, he hated that his girlfriend was in danger again because of him. He'd done everything he could to keep her safe, but he hadn't. He had fucked up not doing more to make sure she was okay.

His phone rang as he flipped on the water to rinse his mouth. The call was from Vine. "Yeah," Dunk said.

"Shit, man. We need to figure out what to do."

"The jerk wants me on a plane. I'm getting dressed and about to leave my house."

"Drive to base," Vine said.

"I need to—"

"Just get to the base. We'll figure something out."

Dunk closed his eyes, trying to gather some sort of composure. "Okay. I'll be there soon."

He pulled on his uniform, wondering what the heck he was going to do. He needed to save Rosalind, but he doubted if he rushed to her side that Lyle would allow them to leave. The man had sounded unhinged.

On the drive to the base, his phone rang. "Hello?"

"This is Tex."

"Oh," was all Dunk could manage.

"I have a guy in an empty house across from her. He can see into the den, the bedroom, the dining room, and the kitchen. Right now, everything looks okay. Both women are safe."

A chill swept over him. At least it was early, and the traffic was minimal so he didn't have to pay too much attention to the road. "Shit, what am I going to do?"

"There are three guys I know in Topanga outside of LA. I called them and told them the situation. They are en route. The police probably wouldn't be happy if they were interrupted, so no calling the police."

Dunk drew in a slow breath. "How well do you know them?"

"We've got two SEALs and a Green Beret. Rocky, Chaos, and Zeke. They'll get the job done, and your sister and Rosalind will be okay."

He felt relief for the first time since he had woken up to the psycho calling him.

"Thank you. I swear I would be dead if I didn't know about you."

"You're welcome. And take care of her once you get her home," Tex said.

"Will do."

The call ended just before he took the exit for the base. When he parked, he saw that Vine and Wig were already there. He raced inside and stopped when he saw Dallas Creed.

"We have you on a flight out that is leaving in thirty minutes," Dallas said as he moved in close. "You're riding in one of the jump seats. I've got MP's driving you. Leave any weapons here. You need to go now. You're not going through the terminal, but you are riding commercial."

"Thank you, sir. I'll never be able to thank you enough."

"Just get her back."

The flight from Honolulu to Los Angeles would take five hours which was way too long for his taste. Just after the doors closed, one of the stewards came over to speak with him.

"Excuse me, sir. There is a seat in business that is open. Could you please come with me?"

"I don't—"

"Nonsense, the pilot insisted. Said he wouldn't take off until you were in that seat."

Dunk stood and followed the man to the front of the business class. He strapped in and settled into his seat, wondering if any progress had been made. No one had called or texted, and now he had to turn off his phone, and he wouldn't have access until they landed in Los Angeles.

CHAPTER THIRTY-THREE

*R*osalind heard Lyle hit Dianna again. He'd been at it for a while. It had been thirty minutes, maybe more, since he'd taken Dianna into the bedroom. Her stomach pitched each time Dianna screamed.

So far, she'd accomplished nothing since she'd been left alone. She hadn't been able to move the heavy chair Lyle had tied her to, nor could she get to a phone or get any of her devices to work.

The first thing Lyle had done was take her phone and turn it off. He'd gone around and unplugged her computers, speakers, TV, anything that might have had a connection to the internet. There would be no yelling at any device to save the day by having a robot call the cops.

She didn't want to think about dying here without

having a chance to say goodbye to Daniel. She missed him terribly.

No doubt, he would be pissed that she'd been taken hostage. Lyle had used Dianna's phone, but she didn't know who he'd called. The bastard had toyed with them for a while, telling her that he had already had Daniel killed. She hadn't believed him, but doubt crept in.

The sounds from the bedroom made her think Lyle had forced himself on Dianna. She didn't want to listen, but her hands were bound, and she couldn't stop the noise.

Tears spilled from her eyes, and her vision blurred. But it wasn't so bad she couldn't see the man in black creeping along her patio. For a moment, she thought the guy was with Lyle. But that didn't make sense.

She watched as the guy moved to the big glass door and slid it open. He lifted his hand to his lips, telling her to be quiet. She gave a quick nod, praying this man was here to save her.

A second man crept inside and moved to her bedroom door. They must have been watching to head to her bedroom door.

The first guy moved to her front door and opened it, allowing another man to enter. The guy who came in through the front began untying her hands.

"Are you injured?" the guy whispered to her.

She shook her head, not trusting her voice. Her arms shook as they came loose. She rubbed her wrists as blood surged, bringing tingles to her forearms and hands.

He moved so she could see his hazel eyes. "Follow me."

She nodded and tried to stand, but her legs almost gave out. In a swift move, he picked her up and carried her outside to a waiting van.

Once she was seated in the van, she met his gaze. "Do you know Dunk?" she asked, fearful this was another guy who would abduct her.

The guy shook his head, and she almost screamed, but his answer reassured her.

"I haven't met him, but we have mutual friends. From what I understand, he's on a plane and headed here. We decided to intervene since he took Miss Wilson into the bedroom."

"Oh." Her eyes went wide. "So you were watching?"

"Yes, ma'am. We've had a spotter watching for a few hours. I've been sitting out here for a while."

Tears poured from her eyes, and she squeaked out, "Thank you." Her whole body shook, and he draped a jacket over her shoulders. "What's your name?"

"Zeke."

"Thank you for saving me."

His cheeks turned a little pink, and she glanced down at her hands. When she looked up, his eyes narrowed. She looked at his ear and saw he had an earbud in it. He must be listening to his friends.

She didn't have time to wonder about anything else

because the door opened, and Dianna came out with one of the men. Rosalind wanted to run to her, but Zeke put his hand on her shoulder.

"She's coming this way."

"Are the police coming to arrest Lyle?" Rosalind asked.

Zeke shrugged. "Best we not talk about what happens to him."

Dianna stepped up into the van, and Rosalind pulled her into a hug. They cried together as the men stepped outside the van.

"Are you okay?" Rosalind asked.

She nodded. "They broke his arm."

"Are they calling the cops?" Rosalind knew Lyle needed to serve time, but she hated that her name would be dragged through this. People would blame her for what happened, and rumors would spread through social media, trade rags, and then back to social media, getting dirtier with each pass.

"I don't think they are. They're giving him a few options, but they didn't sound like good options."

Zeke stuck his head back into the van. "You two all right?"

Dianna bit her lower lip. "I need to pee."

"We have him locked down so you can go back into the house. We're sticking around until Dunk gets here."

Dianna blew out a breath. "Great, my brother is going to hate me. I brought this asshole into our lives."

"Hey, you aren't the one who did anything wrong. Don't blame yourself for this guy's failures."

Zeke was right, but even Rosalind felt guilty that this guy had been able to get in and hold them hostage. If only she'd trusted her gut and not opened the door for him when he'd shown up. She should have told him to go away, but she didn't know.

She heard a phone ring, and one of the guys pulled it out of his pocket. "Hey, is this your phone?" the guy asked.

She spied Daniel's name on the screen. "Yes," Rosalind said as she took a huge step toward him.

He smiled and handed the phone over. "Hello." She still sounded scared.

"Are you okay?" Daniel asked.

"Yes. Everything is good now."

Zeke held out his hand, and Rosalind nodded.

"One of the guys wants to talk to you."

"Sure, put him on."

She handed the phone to Zeke, who didn't take long to say they were all okay. Zeke mentioned two names, Chaos and Rocky. The other two guys waved, and she lifted her chin, acknowledging them.

Zeke handed her phone to her, and she fought the tears that wanted to spill over. "Are you in LA?"

"Yes. It will take a while to get to your place, but I'm coming. The guys are going to stick around until I get there. You're safe with them."

"Thank you."

"Babe, you don't need to thank me. All of this is happening because I fell down on the job."

She shook her head though she knew he couldn't see her. "No, you aren't the reason Lyle did this. He's a bastard. It's not on you."

He blew out a breath, and she knew he would have difficulty getting rid of the guilt. They both needed help to get over things. It was time they took therapy seriously.

"I'll see you in just a bit."

"Drive safe," Rosalind said.

After the call ended, she headed to her kitchen and grabbed a glass of water, offering everyone something to drink. Dianna was the only one to take her up on the offer. After twenty minutes, a car pulled up.

"Is that Daniel?" she asked Zeke.

"No. It's someone who will take custody of Lyle. They've been looking for him for a while."

"Oh. Will he be okay?" Rosalind asked.

"I hope not," Zeke said.

"He's not going to see freedom for a while," Chaos said.

She shivered as Rocky helped get Lyle outside. He looked unconscious based on how his feet were dragging.

"It was my choice what happened. Lyle couldn't pick any of the options they gave him so I did," Dianna said. "I picked something that will keep him away from me for a very long time, if not forever."

Rosalind reached out and pulled Dianna into a hug. "I'm glad you're okay."

Dianna pulled her close. "I will be."

Before the hug ended, the door opened, and she heard Daniel call for her. Her eyes may never recover from this crying jag.

Then she was in Daniel's arms, knowing everything would be good from here on out. After a moment, he stepped away from her and went to each man, shaking their hands.

"I owe you my life," Daniel said.

"You'd do it for us if you could," Zeke said.

"Damn straight."

They each hugged Daniel before they shook hers and Dianna's hands. She had no clue if they were military or law enforcement, but she knew this was probably one of those things she couldn't talk about.

Dianna went to the doctor at Daniel's insistence, but they were safe in her house later that evening when she glanced around and shook her head.

"I can't sleep here."

Dianna nodded. "It's a beautiful house, but don't ever expect me to come back here again."

Rosalind blew out a deep breath. "I guess this place is going on the market."

Daniel squeezed her hand. "I'm good with whatever you choose to do. But first, I wanted to say something."

Rosalind turned to look at him. "What's up?"

"I've decided to leave the SEALs."

"What?" Rosalind shook her head. "No, I can't make you do that."

"Hey, you aren't making me do anything. I've had time to think about it. I know my time is limited. I was released for missions, but earlier this week, I was training, and I fell. Then I missed the targets, and that's never happened. It's time."

"I want you to really think about it," Rosalind said.

"Babe, that's all I've been doing for months. At first, I thought I'd die if I lost my position on the team, but then I realized there are more important things in my life. I'm not mission ready, and that puts everyone at risk. I'm not sure I'd be able to get back to mission-ready status either, and there's something I want to do more than being a SEAL."

"That's a huge shock," Dianna said. "You've never wanted anything more than being a Navy SEAL for years."

Daniel stood then went down on one knee in front of Rosalind. "Now there is. I can't buy you diamond rings or give you golden crowns, but I can cherish you every day for the rest of my life. I think I started falling for you that first week in paradise, and my love for you has only grown. Please marry me."

Rosalind cupped his cheeks. "Yes. I love you, and I don't want to lose our relationship. We've been through so much, and I know our love is real."

He plastered his lips against hers, making her almost dizzy with delight. She had a man who would cherish her forever, and she would cherish him, too. Maybe they didn't know what tomorrow would bring, but they would face it together.

EPILOGUE

*R*osalind and Dunk had waited to get married until his old SEAL team had enough leave. They had flown them all to California and had a private ceremony at a huge ranch outside San Diego. Half the guests were military, and the other half were stars. It was funny to see the mutual admiration, especially when the stars found out most of the guys were Navy SEALs.

"Are you ready?" Dianna asked.

"As I'll ever be." Rosalind smiled at her reflection in the mirror.

"You look amazing."

Rosalind felt giddy as a schoolgirl. "I can't believe the day is finally here."

"I know. How are you going to celebrate?" Dianna asked.

"We're going to spend a few weeks in Hawaii, then head to Australia, where I'm filming my next movie."

Dianna nodded. "Nice."

The door opened, and Rosalind gasped. She turned to see Jenna's wide smile. "They're ready for you."

Rosalind's hands shook as she reached for the flowers. This was the most important role she would ever take on. She had fallen in love with a man she never would have met under normal circumstances, and now she was happier than ever. Daniel was finding his way after leaving the Navy, but he was happy doing security consulting for now. Maybe he would open his own business soon or continue freelancing.

They had a tent set up with a wide cover making it nearly impossible for drones to get a good shot of her dress. Of course, the media had gone crazy with speculation about who Daniel was and why they were getting married, but that didn't matter.

Her sister had tried to weasel her way back into her life, but Rosalind had shunned her, keeping her family at a distance. She didn't need the headaches. It would have been nice to have a sister who she could trust to attend her wedding, but there was no way their relationship could be anything but toxic.

Rosalind hadn't been able to see Daniel until she stepped around the last row of chairs and spied her man. He looked amazing. Vine stood beside him, whispering something that made Daniel smile.

They'd lived together as much as they could over

the last fifteen months, but now, with Daniel out of the military, they would be able to spend much more time together.

The people in the chairs to her left and right were a blur. She only had eyes for her man. She'd thought she would remember every bit of it, but she had no clue who she smiled or winked at. She was just thrilled to be here with Daniel.

They'd opted for shorter vows instead of drawing the ceremony out. A weight lifted from her shoulders when Daniel's lips pressed against hers. She had a husband who loved her.

After more photos, the first dance, and cutting the cake, she stood with Daniel in the middle of the dance floor, swaying slightly as they laughed and chatted. She glanced around and nodded.

"What was that nod for?" Daniel asked.

"Our friends mix well. Just look at them. They all seem to respect each other, though it looks like a few from the younger set of actors are trying hard to hit on a few of the SEALs."

Daniel threw back his head and laughed. "They're all adults. They can handle themselves."

She nodded. "They are. I just wonder if they know what they're getting themselves into."

Daniel lifted his eyebrows. "What do you mean?"

She brushed her lips over his and then moved to whisper in his ear. "SEALs are dangerously sexy, and if you're any indication, their bed game is on point.

Those actors and actresses are going to have their minds blown."

Daniel laughed again. "I can't say if their bed game is good or not, but I do want to show you some of my moves."

She kissed him again, loving how wonderful being with him was. They had gone through hell to get to where they were. She wouldn't trade it for the world. Daniel had saved her from a mediocre existence. Now every day was amazing, all because she'd found her SEAL.

OTHER BOOKS BY JULIA BRIGHT

ABOUT THE AUTHOR

Julia Bright is the author of the contemporary military romance Dark Eagle series and is an Operation Alpha Author. Julia lives in the south where "bless your heart" is an insult and "shut up" shows love. Julia has been reading since they could open a book and has taken the passion for words and combined it with the love of travel to create stories full of passion and excitement. If you love a good book with a fantastic happily ever after, you'll enjoy a Julia Bright novel. For a dash of paranormal romance and urban fantasy, pick up a book from Julia's USA Today Bestselling JS Bright pen name

f facebook.com/AuthorJuliaBright
a amazon.com/Julia-Bright/e
BB bookbub.com/authors/julia-bright

There are many more books in this fan fiction world than listed here, for an up-to-date list go to www.AcesPress.com

You can also visit our Amazon page at:
http://www.amazon.com/author/operationalpha

Special Forces: Operation Alpha World

Christie Adams: Charity's Heart

Linzi Baxter: Unlocking Dreams

Misha Blake: Flash

Anna Blakely: Rescuing Gracelynn

Julia Bright: Saving Lorelei

Cara Carnes: Protecting Mari

Kendra Mei Chailyn: Beast

Melissa Kay Clarke: Rescuing Annabeth

Samantha A. Cole: Handling Haven

Lorelei Confer: Protecting Sara

KaLyn Cooper: Spring Unveiled

Janie Crouch: Storm

Jordan Dane: Redemption for Avery

Tarina Deaton: Found in the Lost

Riley Edwards: Protecting Olivia

Dorothy Ewels: Knight's Queen

Lila Ferrari: Protecting Joy

Nicole Flockton: Protecting Maria

Hope Ford: Rescuing Karina

Amy Gamet: Guarded by the SEAL

Michele Gwynn: Rescuing Emma

Desiree Holt: Protecting Maddie

Jesse Jacobson: Protecting Honor

Rayne Lewis: Justice for Mary

Callie Love & Ann Omasta: Hawaii Hottie

JM Madden: Rescuing Olivia

A.M. Mahler: Griffin

Ellie Masters: Sybil's Protector

Trish McCallan: Hero Under Fire

Rachel McNeely: The SEAL's Surprise Baby

KD Michaels: Saving Laura

Olivia Michaels: Protecting Harper

Annie Miller: Securing Willow

Keira Montclair: Wolf and the Wild Scots

MJ Nightingale: Protecting Beauty

Melinda Owens: Betraying Katie

Victoria Paige: Reclaiming Izabel

Danielle Pays: Defending Sarina

Lainey Reese: Protecting New York

KeKe Renée: Protecting Bria

TL Reeve and Michele Ryan: Extracting Mateo

Deanna L. Rowley: Saving Veronica

Angela Rush: Charlotte

Rose Smith: Saving Satin

Lynne St. James: SEAL's Spitfire

Sarah Stone: Shielding Grace

Jen Talty: Burning Desire

Reina Torres, Rescuing Hi'ilani

LJ Vickery: Circus Comes to Town
R. C. Wynne: Shadows Renewed

Delta Team Three Series
Lori Ryan: Nori's Delta
Becca Jameson: Destiny's Delta
Lynne St James, Gwen's Delta
Elle James: Ivy's Delta
Riley Edwards: Hope's Delta

Police and Fire: Operation Alpha World
Freya Barker: Burning for Autumn
B.P. Beth: Scott
Jane Blythe: Salvaging Marigold
Julia Bright, Justice for Amber
Hadley Finn: Exton
Emily Gray: Shelter for Allegra
Alexa Gregory: Backdraft
Deanndra Hall: Shelter for Sharla
Jenna Harte: Dead But Not Forgotten
India Kells: Shadow Killer
Amber Kuhlman: Protecting Paisley
Reina Torres: Justice for Sloane
Aubree Valentine, Justice for Danielle
Maddie Wade: Finding English
Laine Vess: Justice for Lauren

Tarpley VFD Series

Silver James, Fighting for Elena
Deanndra Hall, Fighting for Carly
Haven Rose, Fighting for Calliope
MJ Nightingale, Fighting for Jemma
TL Reeve, Fighting for Brittney
Nicole Flockton, Fighting for Nadia

As you know, this book included at least one character from Susan Stoker's books. To check out more, see below.

SEAL Team Hawaii Series

Finding Elodie

Finding Lexie

Finding Kenna

Finding Monica

Finding Carly

Finding Ashlyn (Feb 2023)

Finding Jodelle (July 2023)

Eagle Point Search & Rescue

Searching for Lilly

Searching for Elsie

Searching for Bristol

Searching for Caryn (April 2023)

Searching for Finley (Sept 2023)

Searching for Heather (TBA)

Searching for Khloe (TBA)

The Refuge Series

Deserving Alaska (Aug 2022)

Deserving Henley (Jan 2023)

Deserving Reese (May 2023)

Deserving Cora (TBA)

Deserving Lara (TBA)

Deserving Maisy (TBA)

Deserving Ryleigh (TBA)

Delta Team Two Series
Shielding Gillian
Shielding Kinley
Shielding Aspen
Shielding Jayme (novella)
Shielding Riley
Shielding Devyn
Shielding Ember
Shielding Sierra

SEAL of Protection: Legacy Series
Securing Caite (FREE!)
Securing Brenae (novella)
Securing Sidney
Securing Piper
Securing Zoey
Securing Avery
Securing Kalee
Securing Jane

Delta Force Heroes Series
Rescuing Rayne (FREE!)
Rescuing Aimee (novella)
Rescuing Emily
Rescuing Harley
Marrying Emily (novella)
Rescuing Kassie

Rescuing Bryn

Rescuing Casey

Rescuing Sadie (novella)

Rescuing Wendy

Rescuing Mary

Rescuing Macie (novella)

Rescuing Annie

Badge of Honor: Texas Heroes Series

Justice for Mackenzie (FREE!)

Justice for Mickie

Justice for Corrie

Justice for Laine (novella)

Shelter for Elizabeth

Justice for Boone

Shelter for Adeline

Shelter for Sophie

Justice for Erin

Justice for Milena

Shelter for Blythe

Justice for Hope

Shelter for Quinn

Shelter for Koren

Shelter for Penelope

SEAL of Protection Series

Protecting Caroline (FREE!)

Protecting Alabama

Protecting Fiona

Marrying Caroline (novella)
Protecting Summer
Protecting Cheyenne
Protecting Jessyka
Protecting Julie (novella)
Protecting Melody
Protecting the Future
Protecting Kiera (novella)
Protecting Alabama's Kids (novella)
Protecting Dakota

New York Times, USA Today and *Wall Street Journal* Bestselling Author Susan Stoker has a heart as big as the state of Tennessee where she lives, but this all American girl has also spent the last fourteen years living in Missouri, California, Colorado, Indiana, and Texas. She's married to a retired Army man who now gets to follow *her* around the country.

www.stokeraces.com
www.AcesPress.com
susan@stokeraces.com

Made in the USA
Monee, IL
03 March 2023

29087887R10144